Witch Scl
Book 5
My First True Love

Katrina Kahler

Table of Contents

Chapter One

The season was fall and the crisp sunset-shaded leaves surrounded Charlotte like a blanket. She looked down and saw that her feet were bare and with each step the leaves rustled beneath her.

Although she was outside it held the warmth of a summer's day and the floral print sun-dress she wore suited the temperature.

Behind two arched trees up ahead stood Gerty, Stef and Alice, who waved over-excitedly at Charlotte. She waved back before she began to run across to them. A gust of wind flew past her, causing the blue ribbon that was tied in her hair to come loose and flail in front of her. She reached out and grabbed onto it and began to weave it around her wrist, only the fabric kept on coming, until it was now snaked up the majority of her arm.

She looked down at her ribboned arm questioningly and she was about to continue wrapping the ribbon around her wrist, only she realized that there was no more ribbon to thread.

'Charlotte, over here,' Gerty shouted from up ahead, as she waved and jumped up on the spot.

'Coming,' Charlotte shouted back, only her words seemed to get lost in the air.

She looked back down at her arm to see that the ribbon had vanished, only she didn't linger on this fact, as if the ribbon had never existed.

She walked across the leaves, only they didn't crumple beneath her feet any more, instead they popped and crackled like her mouth did after she'd poured an entire bag of Pop Rocks into it.

Charlotte kept on walking forwards, only she didn't seem to be gaining on the others. Again this didn't seem to alarm her, instead she kept on walking until suddenly she stopped abruptly. The leaves blew up from the ground and whirled around her like a mini tornado.

She blinked her eyes and saw that all the leaves had disappeared, revealing the vividly green grass beneath it. She looked up to see that Gerty was standing there, with Stef and Alice just behind her.

'Charlotte, you made it,' Gerty smiled, as she grabbed Charlotte's her hand.

'About time,' Alice huffed.

As Gerty pulled her forwards Stef and Alice stepped aside and a boy with brown hair and wide eyes stepped forwards.

'Charlie,' Charlotte smiled.

'Come on Charlotte, there's not much time left,' he gestured for her to follow him.

'Time left for what?'

Charlie kept on walking, his pace quickening so that Charlotte had to jog to keep up with him. Suddenly the sky darkened and the grass beneath her feet vanished, revealing a black tar like substance that wrapped itself around her feet and tried to pull her down.

'Charlie,' she shouted, as she tried to pull her feet free.

'Come on Charlotte, there's not much time left,' Charlie turned to look at her and gave her a smile, before he turned his head back and then ran off.

'No Charlie, wait. Please wait. Help me,' she shouted, only he kept on running until she could no longer see him.

The black tar had dragged her down into it, so that it now reached her knees. The more she tried to pull herself free the more it seemed to pull her down.

Her wand, she needed her wand. She patted her hands against the sides of her sun-dress, only it didn't have any pockets. She didn't have her wand on her, she was stuck.

A girl with long blonde hair appeared and walked with ease across the tar towards her.

'Please, help me,' Charlotte said, the tar now at her waist.

The girl reached her and peered down at Charlotte, a smirk on her face; it was Margaret.

'It looks like you're in need of this?' she pulled an oak wand from behind her back.

Charlotte reached out and tried to grab her wand but Margaret pulled it away from her.

She took a few steps back from Charlotte before she dropped the wand into the tar and watched as the black substance engulfed it.

'Whoops,' Margaret sniggered, before she turned her back

on Charlotte and walked away from her.

'Please, come back,' Charlotte shouted, the tar now at her shoulders. 'Margaret!'

The tar crawled up her neck and she took a deep breath in before it covered her mouth.

She was falling in a vat of darkness. She tried to scream but it was met with silence.

She landed with a bump on her feet, the crisp autumn leaves were beneath her and all her friends were stood beneath the two arched trees.

'Are you alright Charlotte?' Gerty said, as she stood in front of her.

'I think so,' Charlotte replied, before she walked alongside Gerty over to the others.

'Hi Charlotte,' Charlie smiled.

'Hi,' Charlotte smiled back.

'Come on girls, let's leave these love-birds to it,' Stef rolled her eyes, before she led a waving Gerty and a sulking Alice away.

'It's just us,' Charlie grinned.

'Yes, it is.'

'Shall we go for a walk?' he held his hand out to her.

'Yes, sure,' she put her hand in his and couldn't hide her

smile as they walked hand-in-hand across the meadow of leaves.

The sun grew brighter, far too bright for this time of year. It caused her hair to stick to her forehead and her arms to itch with sweat. She stopped walking and wiped the sweat off her forehead with the back of her arm.

'Is something wrong?' Charlie looked at her worriedly.

'No, no, I'm fine,' she forced a smile.

Charlie's hand slid free of hers as sweat poured from her palms. Charlotte blushed as she wiped her hands against her dress, only the sweat didn't go away, instead it grew worse, streaming out of her pours like a river until soon both her and Charlie were floating in it.

Charlotte opened her mouth to say Charlie's name, only her word was muffled by the sweaty water. She forced her head above the water as she glanced over at Charlie who had drifted further away from her and who she could see was battling with the water. The boy she liked was drowning in a river of her own sweat. This was bad, very, very bad.

The sweat water vanished and she found herself back in Miss Moffat's Academy, in the great hall. She was relieved to see that Charlie was there, along with most of the girls from her class.

'Charlie,' she said, only as she spoke a pink frosted cupcake flew out of her mouth and hurtled over to Alice like a Frisbee, hitting her in the face.

'I'm sorry,' Charlotte said and this time two more cupcakes flew out of her mouth and hit Gerty and Demi.

Charlotte quickly placed her hands over her mouth and looked around the room. The others were now circling her, smiles on their faces as they eagerly waited for the game to continue.

She couldn't hold on any more, the pressure was just too strong. She couldn't help but move her hands and her mouth immediately opened, causing dozens of cupcakes to hurtle out of her mouth and fly at people. Stef and some of the others managed to duck in time whilst others were hit on the arm and the head. Chuckles filled the room, chuckles that were aimed at her expense.

The cupcakes kept on flying out of her mouth and she looked on horrified as a glittery blue frosted cupcake was spinning its way over to Charlie. The cupcake smacked into the side of his head, covering his hair and part of his face. He looked directly over at Charlotte, the welcoming look on his face had now changed into a look of disgust.

An enormous fart echoed through the room, it was so powerful that it caused the entire room to spin. Charlotte found herself whirling around the room, surrounded by cupcakes…and Charlie, he was there too, looking over at her.

She tried to swat the cupcakes away but the vortex that now surrounded her was too strong. Charlotte let out a loud scream, Charlie looked over at her and soon he was screaming too, so that their shrieks combined together.

It was just her scream left, her single high-pitched scream as she was left alone in this vortex of cupcakes in a place in time that she didn't understand.

'Charlotte, Charlotte,' a far off familiar voice said.

9

Water, swirling, frosting and the sound of her name being called were all that currently existed.

'Charlotte, wake-up,' the familiar voice said, as gentle hands shook her.

Charlotte blinked open her eyes and three blurry figures leaning over her came into her view.

'W-what? Where am I?' Charlotte looked around her feeling confused.

'You're in your room, it's us,' Gerty said.

'You had one heck of a nightmare, it woke us all up. I'm surprised it didn't wake-up the entire Academy. Whatever you were dreaming about must have been bad,' Stef said.

'Well I'm glad you're awake,' Alice sighed. 'But I need at least eight hours of non-interrupted sleep else it is bad for my complexion and my mind. I refuse to take responsibility if I am late for lessons tomorrow, you can take the blame for it.'

'Shut-up Alice,' Stef grunted. 'It's not like she chose to have a nightmare.'

Alice huffed before she shuffled her way over to her bed.

'You're so sweaty,' Gerty said, as she swiped a strand of Charlotte's hair out of her face.

The word 'sweaty' was all it took for Charlotte to sit up with a start and put her hands to her face. Her forehead was damp with sweat but at least she wasn't swimming in it like she had been in her nightmare.

'Are you okay?' Stef asked.

Charlotte nodded and forced a smile.

'Thanks for waking me up, like you said it was just a silly nightmare. I'm glad it wasn't real though.'

'I'm glad it wasn't either, from your screams it sounded like it was a terrifying one,' Stef grinned.

Gerty perched on the edge of Charlotte's bed and Stef copied her. They just sat there in silence for a few minutes and Charlotte was glad that they were there.
Soon snoring sounds came from Alice's bed which caused the girls to exchange looks as they giggled.

"At least she's getting her beauty sleep,' Stef snorted.

'Do you think she realizes how loudly she snores?' Gerty whispered.

'I think we should record it and play it back to her when she's irritating us.'

'Stef,' Gerty gave a disapproving look.

'What, I'm just kidding,' she smirked.

'Thanks guys but I think I'll be okay now. You two should go and get some sleep, just don't snore,' Charlotte smiled.

'Okay,' Stef stood up. 'If you need me you know where I'll be,' she said, before she headed across to her bed.

'Are you sure you're okay?' Gerty whispered to her.

'Yes thanks Gerty, I'm fine now.'

'It's scary isn't it how real dreams can seem sometimes. I once had a dream that my hair turned green and that whatever spell I used to try and turn it back to normal only made it greener. I checked the mirror about twenty times in a row when I woke up, just to make sure that it was still blonde,' she patted down her hair.

'Your hair looks lovely and in no way green,' Charlotte smiled. 'Thank you for looking after me.'

'That's what friends are for. Now, are you sure you'll be okay?'

'Yes thanks Gerty, I'm okay now,' she nodded as she looked at Gerty.

Gerty jumped up from the bed and half-walked, half-skipped over to her bed.

'It wasn't real, it was just a silly dream,' Charlotte whispered to herself, as she looked up at the ceiling.

She didn't want to close her eyes as she never wanted to enter that nightmare world ever again.

***

It took Charlotte ages to fall back to sleep and when she finally did, it had felt to her like the bell signalling the start of the day had rung out almost immediately. She rubbed her tired eyes, got dressed and trailed behind the others towards breakfast, glad that there wasn't a fitness lesson this morning and hoping that eating something would make her feel less like a zombie.

12

'Are you okay?' Gerty stepped back and walked alongside Charlotte.

'Yes thanks, I'm just tired,' she forced a smile.

'You'll sleep better tonight, I'm sure of it.'

'Thanks Gerty, I'm sure I will,' she replied, not wanting to admit that falling asleep easily was what she was afraid of.

As soon as they stepped into the hall for breakfast Charlotte felt like she'd been transported back into her nightmare. Sitting at their table was a pretty girl with long blonde hair; it was Margaret. No one was sitting near her, but this didn't stop the rest of the students in the room from glaring over at her as they gossiped about her.

'What is she doing in my seat?' Alice grunted.

'Maybe she forgot that it was your seat Alice, she hasn't been at this Academy in a while,' Gerty said.

'As if,' Stef snorted. 'Margaret is many things but stupid is not one of them.'

'What do we do now?' Charlotte said, trying to hide the upset in her voice.

Margaret looked up from her breakfast and gave them an enthusiastic wave.

'It looks like we're going over there,' Stef gave an over-the-top wave back, before she grabbed Charlotte and Alice's arms and dragged them forwards.

'Hi,' Margaret smiled, as they sat down next to her.

'Hi,' Gerty said.

'Yeah hi,' Stef muttered.

'So you're back for good then?' Gerty asked, as she grabbed some berries off the plant in the middle of the table and put them into her bowl.

'Yes I am,' Margaret smiled back at her. 'I just hope there's no hard feelings between us, I would like a fresh start and it would be really good if we could all be friends.'

'Sure,' Gerty said.

''We'll see,' Stef rolled her eyes.

'You're in my seat,' Alice muttered.

'What was that Alice?' Margaret asked.

'Nothing,' she blushed as she looked into her bowl.

'I'm surprised you didn't sit with Demi,' Stef glanced over at the table where Demi and Destiny were sitting opposite each other, lost in conversation together.

'It appears that she's moved on,' Margaret gritted her teeth. 'Not to worry, as I said before, I'd love it if we could all be friends,' she smiled. 'What do you think Charlotte?'

Charlotte's eyes grew wide in horror. She didn't want to be friends with Margaret, she didn't want to be anywhere near her. This was the girl who nearly got her expelled and then turned her into a cockroach. She knew that there was absolutely no way that they'd ever be friends.

'I know that I was horrible to you before and I'm truly sorry about that. I just wanted to fit in and I thought that acting how I did would be the way to do that. I know that was daft and I was a cow, but I do want to be friends with you, if you'll forgive me?'

Charlotte didn't know how to respond but she knew that she needed to say something, as all of the girls around the table were staring at her.

'Sure,' she muttered, before she scooped up a huge spoonful of cereal and put it into her mouth so that she had an excuse not to say anything else.

'Great, I'm sure we'll soon all be the best of friends,' Margaret gleamed, the hint of a smirk on her face.

'So Margaret, you don't plan to be flipping burgers in your future?' Alice chimed.

Stef gave her an unimpressed look, before she kicked her under the table.

'Ow,' Alice groaned.

'No Alice, I don't,' Margaret held her smile. 'I plan to work hard and get good results so that I can have a successful career as a witch. Perhaps one day I will be running this Academy.'

An awkward silence fell across the table and Charlotte chewed on the side of her lip. She wanted to finish her breakfast and to get out of there, as being around nice Margaret was making her feel uneasy.

'I better get going, I'll see you in class,' Margaret gave them a wave as she stood up and left the room.

'Do you think we somehow fell into Charlotte's nightmare?' Stef said.

"I was beginning to think that I hadn't woken up,' Charlotte said and Stef leaned over and pinched her arm.

'Ow,' Charlotte uttered. 'Oh no, I'm awake.'

'It sucks to be us,' Stef sighed.

'Maybe Margaret meant what she said,' Gerty said.

'Gerty, I love how you always see the good in every situation but I fail to believe there is any good in Margaret,' Stef added.

'If she wanted to be nice she wouldn't have sat in my seat, she did that on purpose,' Alice said.

'We definitely need to be wary of her,' Stef looked at Charlotte and she nodded.

Charlotte remained quiet as they left the hall and headed towards their first class of the day. When Charlotte had appeared at their Save the Princess party she'd hoped that this had been a one-off visit. None of them had spoken to her then, not even Demi who'd run off into the Academy after seeing her.

No one wanted Margaret back, they'd all been getting on well together and the atmosphere was far better without her around. She was back though and it appeared that she wasn't going anywhere. Still, Charlotte knew that however overly friendly Margaret acted that it was highly unlikely that she meant it.

They walked into potions class to a waving Margaret sitting on a seat on the row behind them.

'At least she's not sitting in my seat this time,' Alice said, as she walked over to the front row.

'This is getting old,' Stef groaned. 'Keep your friends close and your enemies closer,' she grinned, as she waved back at Margaret.

When Charlotte had been five a girl had pushed her over in the playground and she'd grazed her knee. When Charlotte had told her mom what had happened she'd told her that tomorrow she should go up to the girl and ask her to play because no one was all bad. Charlotte didn't imagine that the girl could ever have been nice but she decided to do as her mom said, so the next day she went up to the girl and asked her to play. The girl didn't scowl or shove her over, instead she smiled. After that the two of them became friends and the grazed knee incident was never mentioned again.

As uneasy as Charlotte felt about Margaret's return she knew that she was here to stay and that she would just have to accept this. Maybe if she gave Margaret a chance then she would surprise her, after-all no one could be all bad, could they?

***

The next few weeks passed by in a blur of potions, lessons and books. The other students no longer stared and gossiped at Margaret as they passed her in the hallways or saw her at meal time. The routine of Academy life carried on and with it Margaret mainly kept to herself and remained friendly towards them. Charlotte was still wary of her but hoped that the nasty version of Margaret was gone for good.

All the first year girls were sitting on rows of seats in the great hall talking loudly amongst themselves. They had been instructed to all meet there, dressed in clothes suitable for the outdoors. Molly stood on the stage in front of them, her blonde hair pinned up into a neat bun and her wand gripped tightly in her right hand.

'What do you think we're here for?' Gerty asked, as she sat in-between Charlotte and Stef.

'I dunno,' Stef shrugged. 'I hope it's something good, like another school dance or something.'

'That'd be good Stef but there's only first years here and we aren't dressed for that,' Charlotte said.

'Maybe they're telling each year individually and they have another treat lined up for us afterwards, something happening outside?' Gerty said.

'Silentium,' Molly flicked out her wand.

Stef was moving her mouth to speak but no words came out. She exchanged looks with Charlotte and Gerty before she looked up at Molly. No one else in the room was able to talk besides Molly, however much they moved their mouths.

'That's better,' Molly smiled. 'You're probably wondering why you've all been called here? Miss Moffat is on her way here to tell you herself. All I can say is that you're all going to like it.'

Charlotte turned to face Gerty, she was about to ask her

what she thought it would be? But as she opened her mouth to speak she remembered Molly's spell and closed her mouth.

The doors to the great hall swung open and Miss Moffat flew over the girls' heads on her broomstick. The girls looked up at her, transfixed by her every move. Their gazes followed her over to the stage where she landed next to Molly.

She stepped off her broom and with a click of her fingers made it float above her head.

'Hello first years,' she said, as she looked around the room. I have some exciting news for you, today there will be a picnic and a scavenger hunt with the first year boys from Alexander's College.'

Gerty and Charlotte exchanged excited looks before they looked back at Miss Moffat.

'Silence, how very odd. I was expecting far more excitement than that.'

'Oh,' Molly lifted up her wand and muttered out a spell as she gave it a quick flick.

The hall instantly filled with excited cheers and giggles.

'That's more like it,' Miss Moffat grinned at Molly. 'You will all be in groups of three and at the picnic you will be joined by a group of three boys. You can choose who you would like to be in a group with, so please, go ahead and pick,' she gestured across the room.

Gerty, Stef and Charlotte instantly grabbed each other's

hands and the three of them giggled excitedly.

'This is so amazing,' Gerty said.

'I can't wait,' Stef said.

Alice burst into tears that reddened her cheeks. Charlotte looked from Alice to Stef and Gerty before she chewed on the side of her lip.

Stef looked directly at Charlotte and shook her head but Charlotte ignored this.

'It's okay Alice, you can take my place,' Charlotte reluctantly stood up.

Alice wiped her nose onto the back of her cardigan sleeve and beamed as she took Charlotte's seat.

'Do you think we could have a group of four?' Gerty said.

'I doubt it,' Stef huffed as she crossed her arms. 'Besides, we had a great group of three a minute ago.'

'It's fine Stef, I'll just join another group,' Charlotte said.

'You shouldn't have too,' Stef muttered.

'Right girls, if any of you aren't in a group of three please step out to the front,' Molly said.

Charlotte moved past the other girls and walked out to the front, along with a girl called Cindy, who gave an awkward smile to Charlotte before she pulled on one of her brown-haired pigtails. Charlotte was wondering how it would work if there were only two of them left, when she heard footsteps coming from behind her and turned to see Margaret walking towards the front.

'Great, you three can make a group,' Molly smirked.

'I can't wait,' Margaret looked at Charlotte, her smile forced.

Charlotte gave a faint smile back, knowing that she was stuck in this group now so she had no choice but to get on with it. She thought about Charlie and how she'd hopefully be able to see him soon and her smile grew wider.

'It's so great that the three of us are in a group together, I can't wait to get there. I hope the boys in our group will be cute, do you think they will? I hope we win the scavenger hunt, what do you think the prize will be?' Cindy spluttered out. 'This is so exciting, we are so lucky to be in a group together and I cannot wait,' she said without pausing.

Charlotte smiled at Cindy but Margaret just rolled her eyes and looked away.

Chapter Two

They had followed Molly on their broomsticks until the Academy was out of sight. This was the furthest that most of the girls had even flown before and they felt a mixture of excitement and nerves. Charlotte made sure to keep a strong grip on her broomstick and not to sway too much.

Eventually Molly began to descend and signalled for them to copy her, as she swooped down towards a mass of green. They all landed relatively smoothly, apart from Alice who landed too abruptly and fell head first onto the grass. She instantly stood up and brushed down her grass-stained tights.

Behind Molly were different colored blankets that were spread out across the park. Charlotte looked around for the boys but they hadn't arrived yet.

'It appears as though we are here first. Please can each group go and sit on one of the blankets and await the boys,' Molly said.

Gerty and Stef gave Charlotte a wave as they walked over to a white blanket with blue and red polka dots on it. Charlotte wanted to sit on the blanket next to them but Margaret had walked straight past it.

'This one, purple is my favorite color,' Margaret smirked, as she knelt down on a dark purple and black squared blanket.

'I like purple too,' Cindy said, as she sat down next to Margaret.

'Great,' Margaret said snidely.

Charlotte looked back at Stef, Gerty and Alice who were only just visible from across the park, before she reluctantly sat down on the blanket.

There was a woven picnic basket in the middle off the blanket. Cindy opened it and took out a handful of chips, shoving them one-at-a-time into her mouth.

Margaret pulled the basket towards her and swung back the lid, revealing a basket full of savoury foods and fancy cakes. She picked up a slice of pizza and nibbled on the end of it, before she pulled an empty mug out of it. She picked up her wand and was about to use it…but before she could a sweet smelling liquid bubbled up in the mug, complete with whipped cream and mini marshmallows on top of it.

'Is that hot chocolate? That's so cool,' Cindy pulled on one of her pigtails before she yanked the basket away from Margaret.

'I've not finished with it yet,' Margaret snapped, as she snatched the basket back.

Charlotte looked over at Gerty, Stef and Alice longingly. She imagined Stef stuffing her mouth with cakes as Alice made some comment about how they weren't as good as the cakes she had handmade for her back home, whilst claiming all the strawberry-iced ones.

When Margaret and Cindy had both taken what they wanted from the basket, Charlotte took out a yellow-iced cake and a mug. She watched as it filled itself up and then blew on it before she took a sip. The milky taste of chocolate filled her mouth and for a couple of seconds she forgot where she was. That was until Margaret sniggered at something Cindy said and the realization hit Charlotte…she was in the park waiting for Charlie but she wasn't sitting with her friends. Instead she was sitting with a girl who tried too hard to impress others and a girl who had turned her into a cockroach.

There was a flash of light, so bright, that Charlotte shielded her face with her arms. She cautiously lowered her arm and looked out across the park. The bright light had vanished but the boys had arrived.

'Look, they're here, they're here,' Cindy grabbed onto Charlotte's arm.

'Yes they are,' she forced a smile, as she gently tried to pull her arm free.

They all peered excitedly over at the boys and Charlotte scanned her eyes over them until she found a cute boy with brown hair and wide eyes.

The boys went off in different directions and joined the girls on their blankets. Charlotte saw a group of boys sit down on Stef, Gerty and Alice's blanket and she could tell from his neat black hair that one of them was Benjamin, the boy that Alice liked. Charlotte could just make out that Nick, the boy that Stef liked was also sitting with them and she hoped that Gerty would get on with the other boy.

Charlotte felt herself tense up as a group of three boys walked towards their blanket. She kept a smile on her face, although she tried not to make eye-contact with the boys as she didn't want them to sit with them, instead she wanted Charlie to see her and come over.

Charlie spotted Charlotte and smiled over at her as he gave her a wave. She gave him a wave back and Margaret saw the exchange between them both and couldn't hide her smirk. The group of boys were nearly at the blanket now and on seeing this Charlie weaved his way around the blankets and over to theirs, his wand raised and he was just about to cast a spell but Margaret beat him to it.

'Cadent,' Margaret discreetly flicked her wand at the nearest boy from the group of three that were heading towards their blanket. The boy slipped backwards and caused the two boys behind him to tumble too, like standing dominoes.

Charlie whizzed past the fallen boys and quickly knelt down next to Charlotte.

'Hi,' he smiled at her.

'Hi,' she smiled back.

'Hey, we were clearly going to sit with them,' one of the fallen boys said, as he stood up and glared at Charlie.

'Sorry Doug but I got here first. Although there are still two spaces left.'

'No thanks,' Doug snarled, before he followed his friends over to the blanket where Patricia was sitting with Victoria and another girl.

'Denis, over here,' Charlie shouted over to a frumpy boy, who wheezed as he walked over to them.

Once Denis had caught his breath he proceeded to high-five everyone on the blanket and Charlotte saw Margaret wipe her hand on a napkin after her high-five.

'Hi, I'm Denis,' he said, his accent English.

'Hi, I'm Cindy,' she smiled at him, as she tugged on one of her pigtails.

'Hi Denis, I'm Charlotte.'

'Charlie, you've definitely picked the prettiest girls,' Denis blushed.

'I know,' Charlie grinned, as he looked straight at Charlotte.

'Charlie isn't it? I'm Margaret,' she said, as she knocked into Charlotte's side, extending her hand out to him.

'Yeah, it is. Nice to meet you Margaret,' Charlie shook her hand.

'We're a boy short,' Cindy said, as she looked around her. 'He's cute,' she pointed to a boy standing by himself as he looked for a free spot in a group.

Charlie whistled over at the boy and waved his arm.

'Hey Harry, over here,' he gestured him forwards.

The boy looked relieved as he hurried over to them, only he didn't seem to get any taller as he grew nearer to them. He didn't come up much taller than the rest of the group and they were all sitting down.

'Am I relieved to see you, I thought I was going to be the only one without a group. That would have been more embarrassing than the time I turned my hair blue in potions class,' he grinned and Cindy and Denis laughed.

'You should change your hair to purple, that's my favorite color,' Cindy said and Margaret groaned as she rolled her eyes.

'Anything for you,' he smiled, before he flicked his wand at his hair. 'Purpura tempus.'

Harry's hair instantly turned bright purple and the rest of the group laughed.

'Suits you,' Cindy blushed.

'You look like you belong in a rainbow,' Denis chuckled.

'Or as a candy wrapper,' Charlie grinned.

The purple began to fade until Harry's hair went back to its normal shade of brown and he ruffled his hand through it.

'Is there cake in there?' Denis pointed at the picnic basket.

'Yep there is, oh and I recommend the hot chocolate,' Cindy replied.

'Great,' Denis leaned over the basket and inspected what was inside. 'The cake is great,' he said with a full mouth, so that bits of cake flew out at the others.

'Ew,' Harry shielded himself with his arm. 'Close your mouth Denis.'

'Sorry,' he gulped down the rest of the cake, before he took a bite out of a slice of pizza.

'It's okay, I needed a shower anyway,' Harry grinned. 'Now pass me some of that pizza.'

Denis held a slice of pizza out to him and they both laughed.

'Do you want one?' Denis asked Cindy.

'I'll have one of those little pastries,' she blushed as she pulled on one of her pigtails.

'One of these?' he held an oval pastry out to her.

'Thanks,' she popped it into her mouth.

Charlotte and Charlie weren't taking much notice of what was happening on their blanket as they couldn't stop staring at each other.

'It's good to see you,' he said to her.

'It's good to see you too,' she smiled.

'I like that,' he pointed to the red clip that was in her hair. 'It's pretty, just like you.'

'Thanks,' she blushed. 'I borrowed it from my friend Gerty.'

'I'm so glad I reached you before Doug and his cronies did,' he stared into her eyes.

'I'm glad you did too,' she stared back into his.

'Do you want anything to eat?' he quickly glanced at the picnic basket.

'No thanks, I'm not hungry,' she beamed.

'Me neither, which is a good, as I don't think there's much left.'

Charlotte chuckled, her eyes not leaving his.

As nice as Denis seemed and as funny as Harry was…Charlotte couldn't keep her gaze away from Charlie. She couldn't stop smiling at him and he felt the same, barely taking his gaze off her, a fact which hadn't gone unnoticed by Margaret who folded her arms and smirked to herself.

'Payback time,' she muttered under her breath, a devious look on her face.

Chapter Three

All the groups gathered around Molly and a tall, dark-haired boy from Alexander's College. Charlie was standing next to Charlotte and they kept on exchanging smiles with each other.

'For those of you who don't know me I'm Molly and I'm head girl at the Miss Moffat's Academy. This is Dale, he's head boy at the Alexander's College,' Dale gave them all a wave. 'Each group will be given a list,' she held up a piece of paper. 'And a pen to tick off each item,' she held up a pen.

'Can't we just use magic to tick off the items?' Alice asked.

'Just use the pen,' Molly rolled her eyes, as she began to hand out the lists to the groups.

'As you can see, there are a number of items on your lists, your group's aim is to find them all and get back here first. Whichever group does that and has the most correct answers wins the scavenger hunt,' Dale said.

'What do we win?' a boy asked.

'Win and you'll find out.'

'Are you all ready?' Molly asked the groups, as she stood back by Dale.

There were excited murmurs and nods in reply and Charlie reached out and grabbed Charlotte's hand, which caused her heart to jolt and she couldn't hide the huge smile from her face.

'I said are you all ready?' she said and the crowd responded with loud cheers and whoops.

'Go on then,' she shouted, as she shooed them away.

All the groups instantly hurried off in different directions and Charlotte was led along by Charlie who was still gripping her hand.

'Where first?' he asked Margaret, who was holding the items list.

She looked at his hand wrapped around Charlotte's before she gave a large fake smile at them.

'This way,' she spun on the spot and knocked into Charlotte, causing her to let go of Charlie's hand.

'Sorry,' she said, as she rushed off across the park.

Charlotte longed for Charlie to grab her hand again but instead he just gave her a smile as he walked alongside her.

'Which item are we doing first?' Denis puffed out.

'You have to find the leprechauns house and borrow a cup of sugar,' Margaret read the first item off the list.

'What does a leprechaun's house look like?' Cindy asked.

'Well it isn't going to be a mansion is it?' Margaret rolled back her eyes.

'I reckon it'll be a small house that's even shorter than I am,' Harry grinned and the rest of the group giggled, including Cindy who made sure that she was walking next to him.

'Let's try through here,' Margaret led them towards the forest area that was at the end of the park.

That'd make sense,' Harry said.

Charlotte was wary about entering a forest with Margaret, but at least she had Charlie with her. She hoped that Margaret wouldn't turn her into a cockroach in front of the others, although she couldn't fully rule it out. Margaret may have been all friendly towards her but Charlotte was still unconvinced, although she hoped that she really had changed as being civil with her was much more preferable than having her as an enemy.

'What's that,' Charlie ran over to a tree and bent down.

'It looks like a door,' Denis puffed out.

'Well spotted Charlie,' Margaret smiled.

'Thanks,' he grinned back at her.

Charlie knocked on the little red door and waited for an answer. It was then that Demi and her group appeared and Demi shoved her way over to the leprechaun's door and pushed Charlie out of the way just as the door opened.

A leprechaun in a green suit and a large green hat appeared and looked up at her.

'Please can I borrow a cup of sugar?' Demi asked.

The leprechaun muttered something under his breath as he disappeared inside the tree. He appeared back with a tiny cup of sugar held out in his hand and nodded as Demi took it, before he slammed the door shut.

'Wait,' Charlie shouted. 'We need a cup of sugar too.'

'And we were here first,' Margaret huffed, as she glared at Demi. 'You cheated.'

'There is nothing in the rules to say we have to be polite,' Demi smirked, as she barged past Margaret and back over to her team.

'Game on,' Margaret glared at her with folded arms.

'Whatever,' Demi rolled her eyes. 'Got it,' she held the cup out in front of her team.

'That's tiny, it's no bigger than your thumb,' one of the boys on their team said.

'Let's get out of here,' Destiny said.

The other team ran off into the forest and Charlotte's team remained by the leprechaun's house feeling frustrated.

Charlie knocked on the door again and waited for a response. Eventually the little door opened with force and the grumpy looking leprechaun stared up at them.

'What d'ya want?'

'A cupful of sugar please.'

The leprechaun slammed the door shut and Charlie looked up at Charlotte.

'Do you think he's coming back?' he asked.

'I hope so, as I refuse to be beaten by Demi and that girl she's found to replace me,' Margaret sighed.

'Don't worry Margaret, I think we'll win,' Cindy said but Margaret turned her back to her.

Eventually the leprechaun appeared and half-gave, half-threw the minute cup of sugar at Charlie.

'Thanks,' he replied, just as the leprechaun slammed the door in his face.

'I thought leprechauns were meant to be cheery old fella's,' Harry said.

'Not this one,' Charlie grinned, as he carefully grasped the small cup of sugar.

'The leprechauns we have at the Academy are always friendly,' Cindy said.

'Yeah, the ones at our College are too. They serve us the best steak and mushroom pie ever, it's even better than my mom's, erm, don't tell her I said that,' Denis said.

'Mrs Jackson, I'm afraid your steak and mushroom pie just isn't good enough,' Harry put on a posh English accent.

'Cut it out,' Denis play hit Harry's arm and nearly knocked him over. 'Sorry,' he very gently patted Harry on the shoulder.

'It's okay buddy, you've got some muscles on you there,' he smiled and Margaret let out a snigger.

'When you've quite finished we have a scavenger hunt to win,' Margaret announced.

'Yeah, sorry, what's next?' Denis asked.

Margaret looked over at Charlotte and saw that Charlie was still standing next to her, they were both staring at each other and it was as though no one else existed.

Margaret clutched tightly onto her wand and gave a

mischievous look.

'What's next?' Harry asked.

'Find a gnome and ask them how do a gnome kiss?'
Margaret replied.

'Okay, let's go!' Cindy began to walk forwards but paused
when she saw that Margaret wasn't moving.

Margaret shooed her forwards and let all of the group pass
her, including Charlie and Charlotte who were too busy
smiling at each other to notice that Margaret hadn't moved.
Now that she was at the back of the group she held out her
wand and aimed it towards Charlotte's back.

'At the mention of their name ventus,' Margaret said,
smirking as she hurried past them.

'Which direction do you think we should take Charlotte?'
she asked.

Charlotte let out a loud fart which seemed to echo around
the group. Her face went the shade of beetroot, desperately
hoping that no one realized that it had been her.

'Who did that?' Harry laughed.

'That's horrible,' Cindy flapped her hand in front of her nose.

'Well it wasn't me,' Denis said.

'You know the saying, whoever smelt it dealt it,' Harry
grinned over at Cindy.

'It wasn't me,' she said defensively.

'Who do you think it was Charlotte?' Margaret asked.

Charlotte instantly let out another loud fart and this time everyone knew that it had been her.

'Sorry,' she blushed.

She couldn't bring herself to look at Charlie, worried that he wouldn't like her any more.

'See, it wasn't me,' Cindy said.

'Or me,' Denis said.

'No, it was Charlotte,' Margaret smirked as Charlotte let off another loud fart.

Charlotte was more embarrassed than she could ever express. She wanted to run off into the trees and be far away from the rest of the group, then she wanted a beautiful white pegasus with a glossy mane and feathered wings to fly down and flick her onto its back. She wanted to be flown high up into the clouds and away from this situation.

As much as she wanted to escape she knew that she couldn't, instead she was stuck here with Charlie who most probably thinking she was disgusting. She felt warm fingers curl around hers and looked up to see that they were Charlie's and that he was smiling at her, so she smiled back.

Margaret was furious, she didn't understand how Charlie could still like Charlotte. She decided that there was only one thing for it, she'd just have to repeatedly say Charlotte's name until Charlie's smile faded.

'Charlotte, I think you should look over there,' Margaret

pointed to the side of her as Charlotte immediately farted. 'Go on Charlotte, before the other teams beats us Charlotte.'

Charlotte didn't understand why she couldn't stop farting but going by the smirk on Margaret's face she predicted that she had something to do with it.

She followed Margaret's instructions and hurried off, glad to put some distance between her and the others, although she still found herself glancing back at Charlie. Sweet, caring, super cute Charlie, she knew that he liked her for her and that whether she farted or not wouldn't put him off. She smiled to herself as she stepped over a large white spotted red mushroom.

'Watch it!' a squeaky voice said.

She peered around to find the source of the voice but couldn't see anyone there.

'Down here,' the voice said.

Charlotte carefully knelt down and looked at the ground, before she spotted a gnome with rouge cheeks and a blue waistcoat standing beneath the mushroom.

'Oh, hello there,' Charlotte smiled at him. 'I'm sorry to disturb you, I was just wondering if you could perhaps answer a question for me.'

'I guess I could, if you promise to take more care where you're stepping in future.'

'I will,' she smiled.

'I was wondering if you could tell me how do you kiss?'

'Kissing hey,' he chuckled. 'I can't tell you that.'

'Please, you said that you woul-'

'But I can show you.'

Charlotte nodded, she lowered her head and closed her eyes, waiting for the kiss from the gnome. Only the gnome didn't kiss her lips, instead he rubbed his nose against hers.

'Now if you don't mind I'd like to be left to my thoughts,' the gnome said, as he hurried back under his mushroom.

'Thank you,' Charlotte waved at him, as she hurried back over to her group. 'I found a gnome and got the answer.'

'That's great,' Harry said.

'Well done,' Cindy said and the rest of the group, except for Margaret, all clapped and cheered.

'About time,' Margaret said under her breath, as she rolled her eyes.

'What's next on the list?' Cindy asked, but Margaret ignored her.

'Come on, we've got to find a pot of gold at the end of the rainbow and take one gold coin out of it,' Margaret said, as she rushed forwards. 'Hurry-up, she shouted back to them.'

'Good one,' Charlie said, walking alongside Charlotte. 'I knew you'd find the gnome and get the answer, you're as smart as you are cute.'

'Thanks,' Charlotte blushed.

'So, what what did he say the answer was?'

'He didn't tell me, he showed me.'

'Oh, well now I'm jealous of that gnome,' he gently grabbed her arm to stop her walking and they both stared at each other.

They both leaned in closer to each other until they were so close to each other that Charlotte could feel his breath brush against her face. Charlotte closed her eyes and pursed her lips, as she waited for Charlie's lips on hers.

'Charlotte, Charlotte, Charlotte,' Margaret whispered and Charlotte let out three loud farts.

Charlie pulled away from her and couldn't hide his laughter. Charlotte covered her face with her hands before she rushed forwards. She had been touching distance away from her very first kiss and it'd been ruined. She wanted to cry, scream and hide all at the same time and she longed for Stef, Gerty and even Alice to be here to cheer her up and give her advice.

Margaret was the first to spot the rainbow and they all followed her to the pot of gold. Charlotte trudged behind them, watching as Charlie caught up with Margaret and chatted to her.

'Are, y-you, okay, Charlotte?' Denis puffed out, as he stopped walking to catch his breath and she farted on queue.

'Sorry,' she blushed. 'It seems as though that keeps on happening to me today.'

'It's okay, it happens to be too, especially after I've eaten beans,' he grinned.

She gave a weak smile and chewed on the side of her lip. Suddenly a realization clicked in her head and she grabbed onto Denis's arm.

'Say that again.'

'W-what, that beans make me fart?'

'No, no, not that. My name. Say Charlotte,' she farted.

'Okay Charlotte,' he replied and she farted again.

'Exponentia remotio,' she said, as she turned her wand on herself.

'Denis, can you say my name again please?'

He nodded and then coughed to clear his throat.'

'Charlotte,' he smiled at her.

'Did you hear that?'

'What?'

'I didn't fart. Charlotte, Charlotte, Charlotte.'

'You think someone put a spell on you?'

'It would appear so.'

'Who would do that?'

'I have a good idea,' she folded her arms and looked over at

Margaret.

'Will you both stop flirting with each other and hurry up,' Margaret shouted over to them.

'Catch you in a bit,' Charlotte smiled at Denis, before she stormed forwards, slowing down behind Margaret and discretely aiming her wand at her.

'At the utter of their name eructate,' she said quietly, before she hurried forwards until she was walking alongside Charlie.

'Charlotte, the end of the rainbow is up there,' Margaret smirked, until she realized that Charlotte hadn't farted. 'Charlotte,' she repeated.

'Why don't you lead the way Margaret,' she smiled back, just as Margaret let out a loud burp. She immediately covered her mouth with her hands and ran off.

'Hey,' she smiled at Charlie.

'Hi,' he smiled back.

They all reached the end of the rainbow where a large bronze pot lay beneath a patch of overgrown grass. It was so overfilled with glowing gold coins that Margaret had to pick one up cautiously so that she didn't knock any over.

'Wow, there must be hundreds of coins in there!' Cindy exclaimed.

'I doubt they'd notice if we took more than one,' Harry grinned.

"We are not getting disqualified because of your greed,'
Margaret snapped.

'Alright calm down, I was only joking.'

'There are no times for jokes, we have a scavenger hunt to
finish,' she huffed, as she held the list up.

'I'd rather spend time with you than have a pot of gold,'
Charlie whispered to Charlotte.'

'Same,' she nervously giggled back.

They finished off the rest of the items on the list and then
hurried to the finish line, where Molly and Dale were
waiting.

The picnic blankets had been moved together to make one
giant blanket that resembled a patchwork quilt and there
was a long table filled with yet more sandwiches and fancy
cakes.

'Wow,' Denis said, as he veered off towards the food.

'Ahem, we haven't finished yet,' Margaret huffed out, as she
grabbed his arm and yanked him forwards, his gaze
lingering on the table.

Charlotte turned her head to see Demi and the rest of her
team running towards them.

'We need to hurry,' she pointed to the oncoming group.

'There's no way that I'm losing to them,' Margaret began to
run, her grip still on Denis's arm and he let out a yelp as he
was dragged forwards.

As they ran in sync alongside each other Charlie reached over and took Charlotte's hand.

'Come on guys, remember that the whole team has to reach us for it to count,' Molly shouted.

Charlotte and Charlie reached Molly and Dale just after Harry and Cindy had. They all looked over at Margaret and Denis and cheered them on. Denis was hunched over, his hand clutched to his side.

I...can't...stitch,' he puffed out.

'We are not losing,' Margaret shouted, as she yanked at his arm. 'Pull yourself together.'

'It hurts.'

'If we lose because of you then you have my word that every time I see you I shall turn you into the most hideous toad imaginable.'

Denis swallowed, a frightened look on his face before he nodded and forced himself onwards.

Demi had nearly reached them now and she pulled out her wand and aimed it at Denis's back.

'Don't even think about it,' Margaret held out her wand.

Demi grimaced as she put her wand down by her side but she continued to run, barging past them both and racing over to Molly.

'Come on,' she shrieked over to the rest of her team, who were all gaining on Margaret and Denis.

'I'm not being beaten, least of all by them,' Margaret huffed, as she pulled Denis forwards.

Denis continued to clutch his side but he knew that he had to keep on going, he didn't want to let his team down and he also didn't want to be turned into a toad.

'Come on Denis,' Charlotte shouted.

'Not much further now, then you can raid the picnic,' Harry said.

Margaret kept on yanking at Denis's arm until he fell onto his knees in front of Dale. The rest of the group cheered as they wrapped their arms around him, except for Margaret who stood there smirking over at Demi.

'Well done, you're the first team back,' Molly said, after they had let go of Denis.

'What do we win? Margaret asked.

'Maybe there is no prize, you just get to bask in the knowledge that you won.'

Margaret's face fell and she found herself clutching tightly at her wand.

'Just kidding,' Molly grinned. She pulled a pile of golden medals out from behind her back and placed the medals around each of their necks before she cheered the rest of the incoming teams on.

'Shiny,' Cindy said, as she held the medal up to look at.

'I suppose this will do as a prize,' Margaret said.

'Well done Margaret, we wouldn't have won if you hadn't helped Denis,' Charlie smiled, as he placed his hand on her shoulder.

Margaret didn't burp on her name being used so Charlotte took it that the spell had worn off. She chewed on the side of her lip and tried not to feel annoyed, after-all Charlie was just being nice, a trait which she liked most about him.

'Yeah, well done,' Charlotte smiled.

'Thanks,' Margaret ignored Charlotte and looked directly at Charlie.

A loud sizzling sound came from behind them and they turned to see that Molly had turned the end of her wand into a sparkler and was holding it up in the air.

'It looks like all the teams are back. Well done to all of you, especially the winning team,' she smiled over at Charlotte and Charlie. 'They are the ones wearing the gold medals if you want to congratulate them. Anyway, it's time to feast, so help yourselves,' she pointed over to the long table. 'Although if all the cherry slices go before I get to them, I will not be pleased,' she smirked.

As most people hurried over to the food table, Stef and Alice rushed over to Charlotte and wrapped their arms around her.

'Well done Charlotte,' Gerty smiled.

'I like your medal,' Stef lifted it up to look at it. 'It's a shame we didn't all get one really, seeing as we all took part. They could have given an extra prize to the winning team.'

'We'll just have to win next time,' Gerty said.

'We might stand a chance if we have Charlotte on our team instead of Alice.'

'Stef,' Gerty gave her a stern look.

'Well it's true, a snail would have been quicker than her. All because her shoes were rubbing her feet or something,' she rolled her eyes.

She wasn't that bad.'

'Pfft, that's a matter of opinion.'

'How's it going with Charlie?' Gerty changed the subject.

'Yeah, okay,' Charlotte gave a wide smile. 'Well, apart from Margaret trying to ruin it for me.'

'How so?' Stef asked.

'Someone cast a spell on me so that every time my name was said I farted,' she blushed.

'What a cow,' Stef chuckled. 'Sorry, it is a tiny bit funny though.'

'Yeah I suppose it is a bit, but it wasn't at the time.'

'What did Charlie say?' Gerty asked.

'He was sweet about it but it was super embarrassing.'

'He clearly likes you Charlotte.'

'Yeah, he's looking over at you now,' Stef waved over at Charlie, who was stood by Harry and Denis at the food table.

Charlie waved back, his gaze settling on Charlotte and they exchanged smiles.

'You should go over to him,' Gerty said.

'We should all go,' Charlotte grabbed both of their arms and pulled them forwards.

"I'm not saying no to that, I want an egg sandwich before they all go,' Stef said.

'The sandwiches are always the last thing to go,' Gerty said.

'That's rubbish, I always go for them first.'

'Well then you're the exception.'

'I want a cake, although I think I'll stay away from the cherry slices,' Charlotte grinned. 'How's it going with Nick?' she looked at Stef.

'Okay,' she couldn't hide her smile.

'I'd say it was going better than okay,' Gerty giggled. 'It seems that it's going well for Alice too,' she looked over at Alice and Benjamin who were sitting close together on the blanket and chatting.

'At least it gives us some peace,' Stef said.

When they reached the table Gerty and Stef went off to get food and Charlotte walked over to Charlie. They both smiled at each other and she tried to think of something to say but her mind was blank, all she could think about was how sparkly Charlie's eyes were.

'Do you want a cake?' he continued to smile at her.

'Okay,' she smiled back.

'I recommend the strawberry cupcakes with the vanilla icing,' he picked one up and passed it to her.

'Thanks,' she took it off him and nibbled at the icing.

'It's not as sweet as you,' he took her hand and smiled at her.

Margaret folded her arms as she looked over at Charlotte and Charlie. She was determined to have ruined things for them by the time this picnic had finished, however many spells it took.

'Flumine of in sudore,' she discreetly flicked her wand at Charlotte.

One minute Charlotte had felt fine and the next she'd began to feel hot, so much so that the armpits of her sweater were dripping with sweat and a mass of it glistened on her forehead. She could feel how sweaty her hand was and quickly pulled it away from Charlie's.

'Sorry,' she muttered, as he wiped his hand onto his trousers.

'It's fine,' he smiled. 'Can I get you a cold drink?'

Charlotte nodded before she took a bite of her cupcake and Charlie rushed over to the end of the table and picked up two glass flutes that were filled with different flavoured layers of fruit juice.

'This should cool you down,' he held the glass flute out to her.

'Thank you,' she took the glass off him and studied the layered colors.

'The orange layers are my favorite,' he smiled.

'I like orange too,' she cringed as soon as she said it.

'Haven't you ever had one of these before?'

'No,' she shook her head. 'We don't have these at the Academy.'

'My mom makes them every Christmas and for special occasions, I always drink too many of them, they are irresistible, much like you.'

Charlotte giggled before she took another sip of her drink.

Margaret looked over at them, not understanding how he could still like her, even after the spells she'd cast on her. She smirked as her mind recalled a perfect spell and she aimed her wand at Charlotte.

'Summa cupiditas,' she flicked her wand.

Charlotte took another bite out of her cupcake and then another one. Soon the whole thing was gone but she was still hungry, so she turned to the table and picked up sandwiches and chips.

'You must be hungry,' Charlie said.

Charlotte wanted to stop eating but her hunger was just too strong. She found that she couldn't stop, instead she had to keep on eating. She began to shovel food into her mouth and then she picked up a chocolate cupcake and squashed it into her mouth.

'That foods not just for you,' Molly appeared by her, her arms folded and her gaze unimpressed.

'Exponentia remotio,' Margaret said quietly, as she aimed her wand at Charlotte.

She immediately stopped eating and quickly grabbed a bunch of napkins off the table and spat the food left in her mouth into them.

Charlotte looked at Charlie who couldn't hide the look of disgust on his face.

'Sorry,' she muttered out.

It was then that she felt the nausea rise in her stomach and the tears began to cloud her eyes so she turned and ran off, not wanting the boy she liked to see her be sick whilst crying at the same time. Molly sighed before she followed her, muttering 'first years,' under her breath.

Margaret waited until Charlotte was out of sight before she walked over to Charlie.

'Do you think I should go after her? I didn't mean to upset her, it's just she was eating so much food and-'

'It's not your fault Charlie, the problem runs deeper than that,' she feigned worry. 'Charlotte's my friend and all, but she's got issues, ones I've told her to address but...' she shrugged.

'What is it?' he asked, concern in his voice.

'She'd be sooo mad if she knew I'd told you.'

'I won't tell her you said anything, I just want to help her. I should probably go and check if she's okay,' he started to walk away but Margaret grabbed his arm.

'Well, you saw how she stuffed her mouth with all that food? That's what she always does every meal time and then she runs off to be sick. Sad really but she's been doing it ever since I met her, it makes meal times at the Academy awfully messy. So you can't go after her because if you saw her being sick she'd be so embarrassed and I know how much she likes you.'

'She likes me?' he smiled.

'Well yeah, like way too much. She mentions you like all the time and she writes Charlie hearts Charlotte in all the covers of her books. She talks as if you're already dating, in fact she's always talking about you. I've told her to calm down but she says that you're soul mates and that she's going to marry you and have twenty children.'

'Right,' Charlie said.

'I know a boy like you would never be interested in her. I mean what with all her eating problems and the way she gets weird over you and everything. Still, she's my friend so please let her down gently,' she placed her hand on his and smiled at him.

When Charlotte had stopped being sick, she cleaned herself

up and then hurried back to the picnic to find Charlie, only when he came into sight he was deep in conversation with Margaret. She took a deep breath and walked towards them, not wanting to give in to Margaret.

'Are you feeling better?' Charlie asked.

'Yes thanks,' she nodded.

'You look very pale, I think you should go and lay down as you don't want to infect us,' Margaret smiled.

'I'm fine thanks Margaret.'

'I'm just worried about you Charlotte,' she couldn't hide her smirk.

On hearing her name Charlotte let out a loud, long fart. She blushed bright red and looked at Charlie who was trying not to laugh.

'Like I said, I don't think you're very well,' Margaret patted her shoulder. 'I think you should go and get some rest before you stink us all out.'

Charlotte was annoyed at herself for not noticing that Margaret had put the farting spell back on her. She wanted to scream at her and to tell Charlie exactly what Margaret was like. She wanted to cast a spell to turn Margaret into a balloon and watch her float off so that she was left to talk to Charlie without any interruptions. There were so many things that she wanted to do but instead she found herself walking away from them.

'Is she okay?' Charlie asked Margaret.

'Yeah, she will be fine, she just needs some time to herself,' she leaned in closer to him. 'She always gets terrible wind after her food binges.'

Charlotte looked back at Charlie and let out a sigh. He was so close to her yet he seemed so out of reach.

'Are you okay Charlotte?' Molly asked, and Charlotte let out a fart.

'Sorry,' she looked at the ground. 'Please can I be excused, I don't feel very well.'

'Okay,' she couldn't hide her smile. 'I'll get Sonya to fly back with you to the Academy. Wait here while I go and find her, I know I saw her around here somewhere.'

Charlotte nodded before she looked over at Charlie. Margaret may have won this time but next time Charlotte was determined not to let her ruin it.

'Exponentia remotio,' she turned her wand towards herself.

Soon Sonya walked over to her, both of their brooms in hand and she passed Charlotte's over to her.

'Sorry for taking you away from the picnic,' Charlotte said.

'It's okay, I've had enough sandwiches anyway.'

Charlotte took one last look over at Charlie before she got onto her broom and followed Sonya up into the air.

She thought about her nightmare, the cupcakes, sweat and the farting. All those things had been in her dream and they'd happened today. This didn't make any sense, it was as if she'd subconsciously known what was going to happen to her. Had her dream been some sort of premonition or a warning?

She noticed how everyone looked so tiny from up there, like dots on a map. The truth was that they were all small in comparison to the world but this didn't make them any less important.

Charlotte knew that she mattered, just as all of the dots beneath her did. The next time she met Charlie she was going to prove to him that even though she was quieter than Margaret and not as cunning or as good at spells, this didn't mean that she wasn't just as important as all of the other dots that were down on the ground. Charlotte knew that she was a kinder, fairer, more caring person than Margaret and that she was the dot for Charlie.

Chapter Four

Charlotte landed next to Sonya in the yard of the Academy. A group of second years were having a fitness lesson with Miss Dread, who was twisting herself into a variety of positions and encouraging the girls to copy them. A few of the girls looked over as they landed but most of them were too busy concentrating on their positions to take much notice.

'Do you want me to walk you back to your room?' Sonya asked.

'No thanks, I'll be okay,' Charlotte forced a smile.

'If you're sure?'

'Yep, I'll be fine,' she nodded.

'Okay then, you should go and rest in your room and then hopefully you'll feel better soon.'

'Yeah hopefully,' Charlotte sighed.

'Don't worry, you'll see that boy again soon,' she said and Charlotte blushed. 'I saw you talking to him, he's a cute one.'

'Yes and thanks.'

'Anyway, go and sleep off your bug.'

'Thanks Sonya.'

'No problem, although I hope I get back before Molly eats all of the cherry slices,' she grinned.

Charlotte waved at her and then watched as she flew up into the air until she became a tiny dot in the sky.

'Come on Clarissa, your left leg needs to come up higher,' Miss Dread said.

'I can't, get it up there,' a girl with long red hair said, as she tried lifting her leg up behind her and ended up toppling onto the ground.

Charlotte clutched onto her broom as she walked through the empty halls. She still felt sick from all the food she'd eaten and she couldn't get the taste of vomit mixed with cake out of her mouth. On the walk back to her room she found that she couldn't stop thinking about Charlie. His hair, his eyes, his smile. Everything about him had her smitten and she couldn't seem to shake him from her mind.

She walked into her room and closed the door behind her. Part of her was glad to be alone but the other part of her wanted a hug from Stef, Gerty and even Alice, even though she'd probably go on about how it was messing her hair up. On thinking about them she found herself smiling, they were her friends and she knew that they'd always be there for her.

She brushed her teeth, changed into her pale pink pyjamas and got into her bed. She buried herself beneath the covers as she thought about the warmth of Charlie's hand on hers, winning the scavenger hunt and how Margaret hadn't changed at all.

Swirling around in her mind was the nightmare, which she couldn't stop thinking about. Had she really had a premonition or had it been a fluke? Thoughts of her sweat covered skin, frosted cupcakes and a constant vortex were spinning in her head until her mind switched off and sleep claimed her.

***

'Charlotte, are you okay?' gentle hands shook her.

'W-what?' she blinked open her eyes and saw Gerty and Stef peering over her.

At first she thought that the scavenger hunt had just been part of her nightmare and she felt relief.

'Sorry for waking you, we just wanted to check that you were okay?'

'Um yeah, fine,' she placed her hand over her mouth as she yawned.

'We looked for you at the picnic but Molly said you'd left,' Gerty said.

Charlotte bolted upright, the nausea feeling in the pit of her stomach returned.

'The picnic,' she muttered. 'It really happened, it wasn't a dream?'

'Yeah it happened, your team won remember?' Stef asked.

'Oh yes,' Charlotte lay back down in bed.

'Are you sure you're okay?' Gerty asked.

'Yes thanks, I'm just tired.'

'More like someone spiked your drink with forgetful powder, it happened to my uncle once, he couldn't remember where he'd placed his best hat for a week afterwards, my aunt was the least bit pleased,' Alice said, as she searched through the draw beneath her bed.

'More like your uncle just forgot where he'd put it,' Stef snorted.

'You won't be laughing when someone uses it on you and you misplace your broom for a fortnight,' she huffed.

'How'd it go with Charlie?' Gerty asked.

'Terrible,' she mumbled out, before she sank further into her bed and closed her eyes.

'Charlotte, what happened?' Gerty asked her.

'Let's leave her alone,' Stef whispered to her, before she led her away from Charlotte's bed.

'Who's stolen my robe, the one with the lilac trim?' Alice folded her arms and glared at Stef and Gerty.

'Why would I want your itchy old robe?' Stef replied.

'I'll have you know that is a designer robe.'

'You could show some manners, Charlotte is trying to sleep.'

'Alice we haven't got your robe, I'm sure it's somewhere. I'll help you look for it,' Gerty said quietly, as she walked over to Alice and knelt down next to her before she began to look through her draw.

'Maybe someone used forgetful powder on you?' Stef sniggered.

Charlotte tried to block out the noise from the room and get back to sleep but it was no use. Soon silent tears were streaming down her face and as much as she tried to wipe them away they continued to drip down her cheeks in clear blobs.

'Is this it?' Stef took a lilac robe out of her draw and threw it over at Alice.

'I knew you'd stolen it.'

'I did no such thing, I was merely looking for my PJ's and I found that monstrosity. I reckon you put it in with my laundry so that you didn't have to wash it yourself.'

'You're a thief,' Alice huffed.

'It doesn't matter Alice, you have it back now.'

'I suppose so,' she glared over at Stef, before she put her robe on over her cream satin PJ's.

A knock at the door caused them all to fall silent and Gerty hurried over to it, opening it to see Margaret standing there.

'Hi Gerty, I was just here to check on how Charlotte is feeling?' she smiled.

'She's sleeping,' Stef shouted.

'She's okay but she's resting right now but I'll tell her that you came by,' Gerty said.

'Thank you Gerty, please tell her that I'm thinking of her and that I hope she feels better soon. Also make sure that she knows that I kept Charlie company in her absence so that he didn't feel lonely.'

'I bet you did,' Stef muttered under her breath.

'Thanks Margaret, I'll pass on your message.'

'Goodnight Gerty, Stef, oh and Alice, I didn't see you there but I love your robe, I'd like to borrow it some time,' she gave an exaggerated smile and a single wave in Alice's direction.

'Of course you can borrow it, any time,' Alice shouted over to her.

'Night Margaret,' Gerty smiled, as she closed the door.

'What a load of rubbish,' Stef sneered.

'I think it was nice of her to check by,' Gerty said.

'Yes, she didn't have to do that. I think she's changed,' Alice said.

'You're only saying that because she likes your stinky old robe,' Stef rolled her eyes. 'Besides, she cast a farting spell on Charlotte to embarrass her in front of Charlie, so it's clear she's the same old Margaret.'

'We don't know for sure that it was her who put that spell on Charlotte. She didn't have to stop by and check on her, I think that was a really sweet thing to do.'

'Whatever,' Stef rolled her eyes again. Gerty and Alice might have been fooled by Margaret's words but she wasn't so easily convinced.

***

The Academy's grandfather clock chimed twelve times yet no one stirred, no one that was except for Charlotte who couldn't seem to find sleep. The clock stopped chiming and silence returned, uncomfortable silence. Even Alice wasn't snoring! Charlotte couldn't decide if this was a good or bad thing, as annoying as it was…at least it broke the deathly quiet.

She wondered if Charlie still liked her and what lies Margaret had told him? She wondered how her dream had been so accurate and she wondered why she couldn't stop over-thinking these things and just go to sleep?

On realization that sleep wasn't going to come any time soon a thought flashed into her head.

'I wonder,' she said under her breath.

She carefully pulled the cover off and crept out of bed. She paused briefly before she knelt down and as quietly as she could, pulled the draw out from under her bed.

'Lux,' she held out her wand and the intricate carvings on her wand glowed orange, along with the yellow light that appeared at the end of it.

She rooted through the draw and held up the small vial of fairy dust that she'd won in Miss Scarlet's class. She had been saving it until she believed that she truly needed it and now seemed like a good time to use it.

Remembering what Miss Scarlet said about using it sparingly, Charlotte took the lid off the vial and gently knocked a small amount into her palm. She blew the glittery silver substance into the air and watched as it sparkled before her. Suddenly the sparkles disappeared and in their place appeared a male fairy, with pale skin and purple hair.

'Hello Charlotte, I'm Zonta and I'm here to help,' he said cheerfully.

'Hello,' she smiled back.

'What would you like to ask me?'

'Erm,' Charlotte said, realizing that she had no idea what to ask.

She chewed on the side of her lip as she hurriedly tried to think of something to ask, something helpful.

'What is wrong with me?'

'I can assure you that there is most certainly nothing wrong with you.'

'Really?' she smiled.

'Yes, in fact you are very special.'

'I am?' she gave a confused look.

'Yes, you possess an ability that few others have.'

'What kind of ability?' she whispered.

'Charlotte my little witch friend. You can read minds.'

'No I can't,' she said louder than she intended and then quickly placed her hand over her mouth.

'Us fairies do not lie, I suggest you try it tomorrow.'

'But how do I read minds?' she asked, but Zonta had vanished.

She carefully shone her wand around the room to check that he'd gone, before she buried the vial of fairy dust back in her draw of clothes and then she crept back into bed.

She found herself over-thinking even more than she had been before she had met Zonta. His words repeated in her head and she contemplated using more fairy dust to bring him back and ask him how she was meant to mind read? She decided against this, as she had to at least try to mind read for herself before she wasted more of the fairy dust. Also Miss Scarlet had told her to use it sparingly so she didn't want to risk overusing it.

Thoughts were swirling in her head in a confused ball until finally and unknowingly she fell asleep.

***

Charlotte woke-up first, about an hour before the bell was due to ring. She used the bathroom before a queue grew for it, got changed into her sports kit for fitness training and then stretched out on her bed and thought about what Zonta had said.

She'd read an article in the paper once about this man who took up boxing for a hobby and a week later had won a major championship. Maybe she really did have this hidden skill and she just needed to figure out how to use it.

The bell went off and the others woke-up and began to get ready for the day. Charlotte looked at Gerty and tried as hard as she could to read Gerty's thoughts; nothing.

'You're up early?' Gerty smiled over at her. 'I hope you're feeling better today?'

'I like waking up early, it means I can have the bathroom to myself without feeling rushed,' she grinned. 'I'm feeling better thanks, my head feels somewhat clearer today.'

'Good point and I'm glad.'

'Did you hear Margaret stop by last night?' Stef asked.

'Yeah, I did.'

'She's faker than the fake designer handbag my cousin Belinda takes with her everywhere.'

'Ew, why would anyway buy a fake designer bag?' Alice shuddered.

'Because not everyone is as rich as you Miss Moneybags. Although the bag Belinda has is faded and peeling off at the seams and the zip keeps getting stuck. She's actually told us all that it's the real deal, as if!'

'I think she was being sweet,' Gerty said.

'Gertrude Baggs, you are the nicest person that I've ever met but when it comes to Margaret you are deluded.'

'I'm with Gerty on this one,' Alice said.

'Don't get me started on you, it's far too early for this,' Stef sighed, before she disappeared into the bathroom.

'I was about to go in there,' Alice huffed.

'Gerty, is it true that fairies can't lie?' Charlotte asked.

'Yes, fairies never lie, ever. They are generally kind in nature but their truth telling has been known to offend some people. In fact, legend has it that they seldom come to this realm because centuries ago the ruler of the magical world asked a fairy if they thought they were a good leader? The fairy told them that they weren't and the ruler became bitter with anger and banished all of the fairies from his land.'

'So they can't tell any sort of lies whatsoever?'

'She's already told you that they can't,' Alice snorted.

'Alice, I was just making sure,' Charlotte replied.

'Nope, they can't lie at all. Not even a tiny little lie. Why are you so curious about fairies?'

'Oh, it's just that I read something about them and wondered if it was true.'

'I like fairies, they are so cute. If I was the ruler I wouldn't banish them, even if they told me that I was the worst ruler in the entire universe.'

'You'd be an amazing ruler,' Charlotte said.

'Aw, thanks Charlotte, I think you'd be a great ruler too. We could rule the land together and fill our kingdom with fairies,' she smiled.

'There would be glitter everywhere, imagine the mess,' Alice said.

'I like glitter,' Gerty said.

Charlotte tried to discreetly look down by the side of her bed and saw specks of silver and purple glitter. She got off her bed and knelt down by it, pulling the draw out as a distraction as she used a clean-up spell on the glitter. She tried not to look as it flew up into the air and was swept across Alice and Gerty's heads and into the trash can at the far side of their room.

'I think fairies are misunderstood, much like Tinkerbell was in Peter Pan. She shouldn't have betrayed Peter but she only did it because she was so afraid of losing him. Besides, she turned out good in the end.'

'I do believe in fairies,' Charlotte grinned.

'What on earth are you going on about?' Alice looked bewildered.

'You've NEVER heard of Peter Pan?' Gerty looked stunned.

'I grew up in the wizarding world, we are far too superior to delve into silly fairies.'

'It's a book and a film, oh and also I saw a stage play of it once.'

'Yeah, we performed it at school, I was one of the Lost Boys,' Charlotte said.

'You played a boy?' Alice looked horrified.

'There were more boy characters in it,' she said, remembering how she had secretly longed to be Wendy.

Gerty was still going on about fairies as Stef came out of the bathroom and Alice huffed at her as she hurried into it.

'What are you on about?' Stef glared at her.

'Tinkerbell,' she replied, before she cast a spell so that her bed made itself.

Zonta had said that fairies didn't lie and Gerty had said that they didn't lie either, so surely that meant that unless they'd been some sort of mix-up, then Charlotte could read minds.

'I believe that I can do this,' she thought to herself, before she looked over at Gerty and tried to dive into her mind.

'I stay out too late, got nothing in my brain. That's what people say, mmm-mmm. That's what people say, mmm-mmm,' Gerty sang.

Charlotte stared hard at Gerty, she was still singing but her mouth wasn't moving.

'Strange,' Charlotte thought as she rubbed her head.

The bathroom door swung open and Alice stepped into the room. Gerty smiled at her before she hurried into the bathroom.

'She could have asked me if I'd finished with the bathroom,' Alice moaned.

'What! like you asked me?' Stef snorted.

'It is absolutely ridiculous that we have to share a bathroom.'

'I'd like to flush her down the toilet,' Stef's words sounded in Charlotte's head. Charlotte looked over at Stef who was ignoring Alice as she lay out on her bed and fiddled with her wand.

'Did you say something Stef?' Charlotte asked.

'Huh?' Stef replied.

'Sorry, it's just I thought I heard you say something,' her words trailed off.

'Baby, I'm just gonna shake, shake, shake, shake, shake. I shake it off, I shake it off,' Gerty sang as she came out of the bathroom, only she wasn't singing out loud, instead she was singing in her head.

'I can do it,' Charlotte said louder than she intended to.

'What can you do?' Stef asked.

'Oh, nothing,' Charlotte blushed.

'I hope Charlotte's okay, she's acting odd,' Stef thought.

She could really do it, Zonta had been right, she could read minds. She felt as though she'd suddenly developed a superpower and she imagined herself in a shiny pink leotard with a sparkly mask on.

'Super Charlotte,' she said to herself, as she shook her head. 'No, it can't have my name in it as everyone would know it's me. Erm, how about Mind Girl?' she thought.

She shook her head as she chuckled and Stef glanced over at her.

'Thought Thrower,' she smiled as she said it to herself.

Charlotte looked over at Gerty who was standing in front of the mirror.

'Will my chest ever grow or will I be totally flat-chested forever?' Gerty thought.

Charlotte looked away from Gerty but still, Gerty's thoughts continued in her head.

'I hope it does grow else I'll look like a little kid forever. It's hard enough being the youngest here.'

There was a part of Charlotte that wanted to go over to Gerty, tell her she looked great just the way she was, and to give her a huge hug. She didn't do this though, because she didn't want Gerty to know that she could read minds. The last thing she wanted was for her friends to be wary around her, so she knew that she needed to keep her mind reading skill to herself.

They left their room and headed to breakfast, passing Molly in the corridor.

'He is so gorgeous, I wish I could spend the day with him instead of looking after these little snot noses,' Molly thought, as she smiled at Charlotte.

Charlotte smiled back, although she wasn't impressed at being called a snot nose.

'I wish I looked like Molly,' Gerty thought.

'I wonder if Molly would swap rooms with me for a week if I let her borrow my designer shoes?' Alice thought.

'I hope Margaret's not sitting at our breakfast table, I'm not in the mood to act nice around that cow,' Stef thought.

As these thoughts popped into her head Charlotte found herself looking from one girl to the next. As they walked down the stairs and passed more people, more and more thoughts filled her head.

'If she says one more horrible thing to me today I will turn her as red as a beetroot,' a fourth-year girl thought.

'I shouldn't have stayed up so late studying,' a second-year girl thought, as she yawned.

'Hi girls,' Miss Scarlett said, as she passed them as she walked into the great hall. 'Only five-weeks, three-days and two-hours until the holidays,' she thought.

Demi and Destiny walked alongside them and they exchanged acknowledging waves and hi's.

'They are so lucky that they don't have to share a room with Margaret. I would rather put up with Alice than her. She's so controlling, just when I'm getting in with the good kids she turns up to ruin my life,' Demi thought.

'They should have put me in with the second-year girls. I look as old as they do, I'm sick of being in the baby class, although at least I have Demi around, so this place doesn't totally suck,' Destiny thought.

Charlotte was enjoying spying on people's thoughts, she saw it as harmless fun and she was developing her new found skill at the same time. At least that was until she walked into the main hall and her head was instantly overwhelmed with hundreds of thoughts.

She put her hands over her ears and stopped herself from screaming. It was too much and she didn't know how to stop them.

'Charlotte, are you okay?' Gerty asked her but Charlotte didn't hear her over all of the thoughts.

She sat down at their breakfast table and closed her eyes tightly, telling herself to block out all thoughts but her own. When this didn't work she began to count back from ten in her head and by the time she'd got to one all other thoughts had gone. She let out a sigh of relief before she took a sip of her grapefruit juice.

'Are you okay?' Gerty gave her a concerned look.

Charlotte took a moment to work out if Gerty had just thought this or said it out loud.

'Yes thanks Gerty, I think I just need to eat something,' she took a syrup covered pancake off the large plateful that was placed in the middle of the table and placed it onto her plate.

'They look good,' Gerty looked at the pancakes.

'They aren't as good as the ones made for me at home,' Alice said, before she ate a forkful of her third pancake.

Stef rolled her eyes as she grinned at Charlotte and Gerty.

'My friends really are the best,' Charlotte thought.

She was glad that she had managed to block out the thoughts of her school mates and that the inside of her head was for now just her own.

Chapter Five

The Mistress of Spells was sitting with her huge spell book opened in front of her, her hair was down and she had a beautiful pearl headband holding her gorgeous hair away from her face. She wore a beautiful gold silk dress and her make-up was exquisite.

All of the girls stared at her transfixed, as they waited for her to break the silence.

The Mistress of Spells hummed to herself as she inspected the shelves crammed full of ingredients beside her. 'I must order some more sandalwood,' she said under her breath, before she turned around to face the class.

'Hello girls,' she smiled. 'Decisions, decisions. What spell do you think we should learn today?'

None of the girls said anything, as they all recalled the last time they'd chosen a spell and had ended up looking like nine-year-olds.

'Come on girls, surely you can come up with something?'

'It's not a spell as such but Miss Scarlet has told us a little about the Book of Dragons and we'd love for you to tell us more about it?' Destiny asked.

An awkward silence fell upon the room as the girls looked from Destiny to the Mistress of the Spells.

'We talked about it all the time back at my old school,' Destiny continued.

'Very well,' The Mistress of the Spells sighed. 'I suppose that it is only natural to be curious about this and if I keep it from you, your curiosity will only increase. It's a dangerous book and in the wrong hands the results could be catastrophic. I shall tell you about it, so that your curiosity is put at bay and so that you understand the perils that this book brings. It is not something to discuss frivolously so after this I don't want to hear it mentioned again.'

The girls nodded, as they tried to hide their excitement.

'I want you to take your mind back hundreds of years. The word was a different place then, fear and violence ruled and the weak were oppressed. A powerful witch named Dabria ruled over the magical world, she ruled heartlessly, using dragons to impose her will over all witches and wizards. Those who dared to oppose her were killed by the dragons, who served her loyally, all of them obedient to her will.

'Where did the dragons come from?' Victoria asked.
The Mistress of the Spells glared sternly in her direction
before she continued with her story.

'A thousand years ago there was a tribe called the Izu who
lived in the harsh Arabian desert. The legend was that the
dragons came from a different world, one many realms
away from the one we live in.

One day when the leader of the tribe was out hunting he
found a nest of eggs in a cave. Intrigued by them he took as
many as he could carry back to his tent. That night he ate
one of the eggs and instantly began to change, his skin
cracked and grew as hard as leather. His tail bone
lengthened and formed into a thick tail, his toes webbed and
long teeth protruded from his mouth. So it is told that he
grew so large that he ripped his tent apart. He wasn't human
any more, instead he had turned into a dragon.

He was terrified at first but relieved to still be alive. He was
consumed by confusion and anxiety, yet above all else he
felt the overwhelming desire to fly and so he lifted out his
arms. The skin had grown from his ribs out to the arms,
forming wings. At first he was unsure and unstable, finding
it difficult to control his body. After an hour he felt
comfortable and even enjoyed the freedom of flying. He flew
over to the cliffs above the oasis where his tribe slept
peacefully.

He sat there for hours, wondering how his family would
react to him. Would they realize who he was or would they
attack him in fear? He flew down and sat near the camp-fire
waiting for them to awaken. Just as the sun began to rise
above the horizon he felt himself softening and changing.
He stood by the firelight and watched himself change back
into a human.'

'Did he change into a dragon again?' Gerty asked.

'Yes, every night when the sun went down and darkness descended. When the sun rose the following morning he returned to his human form. He did not tell his family about this and protected the other eggs that he's taken, hiding them in a small cave high on the cliff face above the oasis.

After many moons had passed, the eggs began to hatch. Four tiny dragons clawed their way out of the eggshell and looked to him as their parent. He fed them, nurturing them as if they were his own blood and giving them as much comfort and love as he could muster. Over the following months he trained them to follow his instructions.

When he felt the time was right he gathered his people, telling them that he had something magical to show them. As the sun set they watched as his body transformed into that of a dragon. His tribe gasped in horror and fell to the ground begging for mercy, afraid that he would kill them. He explained to them what had happened and reassured them that they had nothing to fear. His oldest and dearest friend was the first to rise and walk towards the dragon man. Touching his leather skin, he lowered his head and pledged that he would continue to love him like a brother no matter what. They hugged and slowly other members of his family and tribe came to inspect and touch him.

Knowing that this was a shock to his tribe he kept the other dragons a secret for a few more nights before he announced to his tribe that he had more news and then he introduced the four dragons to them. They were still only small and very obedient and at first the people were fearful, but as their fear lessened, they rejoiced in the honor that had been cast upon their tribe. The people worshipped them and showed them only kindness and love. The dragons were only ever used for good.

The dragon man wrote down all the secrets on how to control the dragons in an old leather book. He called it the Book of Dragons, recording in it the secrets of the dragons forever-more. When he eventually died the dragons disappeared and the book was buried with the dragon man's body in a cave. Eventually the stories of the dragons died off and were no longer passed down from father to son. The legend of the dragons was lost for centuries.

This all changed when a witch called Olga the Dark found the Book of Dragons. She summoned the dragons and now loyal to her they obeyed her every command. These were dark, dark times, ones which are best left in the past,' the sadness was evident in her voice, as she wiped away the tears that trickled down her cheeks.

'Eventually she was defeated by the White Witch, Gwenyth. The dragons were encapsulated within the Book of Dragons and it was sealed with a powerful spell.

To keep the book safe, it was entrusted to two wise and good hearted witches.'

'Why did they tell two witches?' Victoria asked.

'In case one died, as they didn't want the secret to be lost.'

'Do you know the witches who were told the secret?' Demi asked.

'Yes, it was Miss Moffat and myself.'

On hearing this the girls gasped, shocked at how powerful

their teachers were.

Charlotte took in the Mistress of Spell's youthful complexion and had to remind herself that her appearance didn't reflect her real age. Charlotte had no idea how old she really was and what horrors she'd seen. The magical world was a fascinating and welcoming place but it sounded as though it hadn't always been this way.

'It is important for you ALL to remember just how dangerous the Book of Dragons is. The pain that it can unleash is more than you could ever imagine, so it is of the utmost importance that its secrets are never unleashed again. Now, enough about this, it's time to commence the lesson and practice spells.'

No more about the Book of Dragons was mentioned during the lesson, although it remained on everyone's minds.

How I imagine the Book of Dragons looks like...

Charlotte chose to block everyone's thoughts out and focus on the floating spell they were doing. She decided that she would have plenty of time to listen in on people's thoughts after the lesson but during them she needed to be distraction free. She really wanted to become as skilled at magic as Margaret was and that would take a lot of time, concentration and effort.

The class came to an end and the Mistress of Spells dismissed the class in her usual positive tone. There was no mention of the Book of Dragons but Charlotte doubted that her classmates would have stopped thinking about it.

Charlotte trailed behind Gerty, Stef and Alice as they left the classroom.

'One day I will be the owner of that book,' Destiny said smugly, as she walked along the corridor with Demi and Melody.

Melody gave her an uneasy look and Demi couldn't hide her shock.

'It's going to happen but don't worry, I may let you borrow a dragon for errands, seeing as you're my best friend,' Destiny grinned.

'Gee, thanks,' Demi rolled her eyes.

Margaret appeared up the corridor and shoved past Melody so that she could stand next to Demi.

'Hi Demi, that was an interesting lesson wasn't it?' she said cheerily.

'Yeah, I guess,' Demi took a step further away from Margaret.

'Are you off to lunch?'

'Yes, WE are,' Demi grabbed Destiny's arm.

Margaret didn't say anything but Charlotte noticed that she had a sly grin on her face. Curiosity took over and as she continued to walk, she focussed her mind and counted to ten inside of her head. Nearby thoughts instantly filled her head and she continued to follow the others, careful not to draw attention to herself.

Charlotte grabbed onto the wall behind her, shocked at what she'd just heard. She stared at the back of Margaret, Demi and Destiny's head as they continued up the corridor.

'Are you okay Charlotte?' Melody asked, as she walked over to her.

Charlotte nodded, as she forced a smile and let go of the wall.

'Yeah, sorry I just went a bit dizzy but I'm fine now.'

'Let's go to lunch.'

Charlotte nodded again as she walked alongside Melody up the corridor.

'I hope there are meatballs, they haven't had them for the last week so we should be getting them soon.'

'Yeah, hopefully,' Charlotte muttered back.

Stef, Gerty and Alice were long gone, no doubt they were now sat in the great hall wondering where she was. It was her own fault for lingering behind them and listening in on people/s thoughts. Maybe she was better off not delving into minds, as she wouldn't always like what she heard.

'Why am I talking about meatballs, Charlotte's going to think I have an unhealthy addiction to them,' Melody thought.

'I hope there's rainbow jelly for dessert, we haven't had that in a while either,' Charlotte said and Melody gave her a large smile.

Margaret, Demi and Destiny were now out of sight but their thoughts were still vivid in her mind. Thoughts which Charlotte didn't know what to do with, thoughts that made her feel nauseous just thinking about them.

Chapter Six

Charlotte was sitting at one of the far tables in the library. She usually opted for whichever free table was the furthest away from the desk of The Mistress of Books, as their relationship was very much flawed since the 'Margaret incident'.

As she wrote down notes from one of the talking books, she found herself glancing over at the golden door where the Book of Dragons was kept. She wondered what the book looked like? Was it a grand golden book with moving images of dragons on it or a simple leather bound book? She wondered what spells were protecting it and the havoc that could be unleashed if it ever got into the wrong hands?

Charlotte quickly looked away from the door, not wanting the Mistress of the Books to see her looking at it. She chewed on the side of her lip as she looked down at her notes and pretended to read them. Margaret and Demi's thoughts were at the front of her mind and seeing the door made what they'd said feel more real. There really was a book behind those doors, a book that could change the magical world forever, a book that in the right hands could be used for good…but in the wrong hands could be used to carry out the cruellest of actions.

'They were just thoughts, I'm sure they didn't really mean them,' Charlotte thought to herself, as Margaret's smirk came back into her head.

Margaret may have been acting all sweet and innocent but Charlotte knew better than to fall for her façade.

'It will be okay,' Charlotte accidentally said out loud.

'Shh,' the Mistress of the Books glared over at her.

Charlotte sank down in her seat and took a quick look over at dragon handled door. She packed up her stuff and placed the textbook on the shelf that was by the door before she left the library and with it the book that she couldn't get out of her head.

***

The great hall was alive with voices and the clattering of spoons against bowls as the students ate their breakfast. Amongst the first years the hot topic was still the Book of Dragons, a fact which didn't sit well with Charlotte. She made the decision not to listen in on anyone's thoughts but this didn't stop most of the girls from talking about the book.

'Do you think anyone's ever broken the spell and got to the book whilst it's been in the library?' Stef asked.

'I doubt it, Miss Moffat and the Mistress of Spells are such accomplished witches that their spells would be virtually impossible to break,' Gerty said.

'Nothings completely impossible,' Alice said.

'Do you think something terrible would happen to the person who tried to get to the book?' Stef asked.

'Maybe their skin turns bright blue?' Gerty giggled.

'Or they turn into a pig,' Stef said.

'Oink, oink,' Gerty wrinkled her nose.

'They are far too sophisticated to cast such childish spells,' Alice said snootily.

Stef rolled her eyes and Gerty giggled, neither of them giving much care to Alice's comment.

'Charlotte, what spell do you think the Mistress of Spells has cast to protect the book?' Gerty asked.

Charlotte looked up from her bowl and shrugged. She didn't want to talk about the book, she was trying to block it from her mind.

'I don't know,' she muttered, before she purposely shoved a huge spoonful of cereal into her mouth.

'Come on Charlotte, I'm sure you can come up with something?' Stef said.

'I reckon any intruders would turn into ice statues,' Gerty said.

'Imagine the Mistress of the Books reaction if she found someone by the dragon door frozen solid?' Stef chuckled.

'She'd probably use them as decoration for the library,' Gerty chuckled.

'With a plaque beneath them reading disobedience will result in this.'

'As if that would be allowed,' Alice huffed, the hint of doubt noticeable in her voice.

'It was a joke, lighten-up,' Stef groaned.

'Well, it was stupid.'

'It's not my problem that you are too snooty to understand jokes.'

'It's not my fault that your family aren't privileged like mine are.'

'That's it,' Stef kicked Alice under the table.

'Ow,' she kicked back.

'Come on, quit it,' Gerty said.

'Whatever,' Stef muttered, as she stirred her spoon around her soggy cereal.

A flash of light exploded over by the teacher's table and silence fell upon the room as everyone looked over to see Molly standing there.

'Please can all first years stay behind for a special announcement,' she said.

There were cheers of excitement from the first years and groans from the other students.

Charlotte kept on looking at Molly, noticing how the ends of her hair had changed color from orange to a dark blue.

'I wonder what spell she's used on her hair?' Gerty asked.

'No idea,' Stef shrugged. 'Back to more important matters, such as what the special announcement could be?'

'I hope it's another picnic,' Gerty clapped her hands

excitedly.

'I don't,' Charlotte said.

'I hope there's food,' Stef said.

'All you think about is food,' Alice said.

'You can't talk, I saw you smuggle those strawberry cupcakes the other day.'

'I did no such thing,' Alice blushed.

'Whatever,' Stef smirked. 'I hope we get to be in a group of three again and this time it won't get ruined.'

Alice's bottom lip quivered as she sniffed and tried to hold back her tears.

'Stef,' Gerty glared at her.

'Sorry,' Stef grunted. 'Hopefully we will get to be in a group of four this time, if there are groups.'

Alice gave a weak smile but she didn't say anything.

'Whatever it is, I hope it's good news,' Charlotte said.

'And that you get to see Charlie again,' Gerty said.

'Yeah and that. I need to fix things with him after our last disastrous meeting.'

'Do you know that Benjamin's parents own their own private yacht?' Alice said.

'That sounds great,' Gerty smiled.

'Yeah, brilliant,' Stef continued to stir her spoon in her mush of cereal.

Charlotte finished her breakfast and she took a few glances over at Demi and then Margaret. She didn't use her ability to listen to their thoughts as she knew better than to do that again in the hectic hall. Still, she found herself wondering what they were thinking and if the Book of Dragons was still on their minds.

***

Only the first year girls, Molly and Miss Moffat remained in the great hall. Miss Moffat had used a spell to remove all of the food, cutlery and tables from the room and to make the chairs form rows at the front.

'Hello girls,' Miss Moffat smiled. 'I am pleased to announce that today signals the start of the Half-Yearly Witches Test. The test will cover three areas that you have learned so far, flying, speed reading and fortune telling, and casting a spell.'

'Tests, great,' Stef quietly moaned to Charlotte.

'These tests are important but I don't doubt your abilities. Each and every one of you has proven that you are true witches in the making and I am very proud of you all. Now, the five girls with the highest overall result in the test will go on to challenge the top five boys from Alexander's College for the Golden Wand Trophy.'

On mention of the boys there were gasps of excitement from the girls and Gerty squealed as she again clapped her hands.

Charlotte couldn't hide her smile at the thought of seeing Charlie again. Then doubt crept in, what if she had put him off so much at the picnic that he never wanted to see her again? She needed to make sure that she was in the top five girls so that she could hopefully talk to him and put things right between them.

She looked over at Margaret and focused on her as she counted back from ten.

'I hope Charlie makes the top five, although I'm sure he will. I can't wait to see him again,' Margaret thought.

Charlotte scowled, as she blocked out any more of Margaret's thoughts and concentrated on Miss Moffat.

'I thought that would interest you,' Miss Moffat grinned. 'But it is also important that you all try your best. Also it would be lovely to have the Golden Wand Trophy in our awards cabinet, which we all know is where it belongs.'

'Even though Alexander's College won last time,' Molly added.

'Yes, thank you for that Molly. The boys may have won last time but that doesn't mean that they won't be beaten this time. I have my faith in my girls and their clear ability to show those boys how skilled we are.

'The first test will begin in two days, so until then my advice would be to practice as much as you can. Don't just focus on your strongest area, as to make the top five you will need to get a high overall score. Remember that a true witch never stops learning and always seeks to find knowledge wherever they can.'

'Don't forget that I expect the top five girls to bring home the trophy, there is a gap in the cabinet that it would fill perfectly,' she smirked, before she gripped onto her broomstick and flew over the girls' heads and out of the great hall.

'Okay girls, I suggest you hurry to class,' Molly said.

All the girls stood up and hurried across the room, none of them wanting to get on Molly's dark side.
'This is so cool,' Gerty jumped on the spot. 'I hope I make the top five.'

'I don't see why you won't,' Charlotte said.

'I hope we all make it, how great would that be?'

'Of course we'll make it, although I'm not so sure about Alice,' Stef said.

'Ahem,' Alice folded her arms.

'Joking,' Stef grinned.

'If we all practice lots and test each other then we'll all make the top five. This is going to be so great,' Gerty looped her arms through Charlotte and Stef's.

'Yeah, it is,' Charlotte replied, unable to hide the doubt from her voice.

She hoped that Gerty was right and they would all make the top five, preferably without Margaret. Then all her friends would be happy and she could hopefully try and fix things with Charlie.

As much as she tried to remain positive there was a hole of doubt positioned in her gut that seemed to be increasing in size the more she thought about it.

***

The next two days were filled with endless practice. By the time the first test had arrived Charlotte had clocked up hours of flying practice, gone to Miss Zara's after school fortune-telling lesson and cast at least a couple of hundred spells. Her hands, mind and wrist all ached, yet she found herself worrying if she had done enough.

The last two days had proven to her just how much she wanted to make the top five, not just for Charlie (although she couldn't deny that she longed to see him) but most of all for herself. She saw this competition as a good way of proving to everyone that although she was brought up oblivious to the magical world, this didn't mean that she didn't deserve to be here.

The test day arrived and a spell of cold weather came with it. All of the first year girls stood in the flying arena, in front of a cheery looking Miss Firmfeather.

In front of them where the rest of the arena should be was a vast whiteness of nothing. At first Charlotte didn't know what was going on but them she came to the conclusion that a spell had been put onto it.

It was a particularly cold morning and frost sparkled on the ground. Charlotte had her warm quilted jacket on over her zip-up top and jogging pants, yet she still felt the cold.

'Waiting in this weather is ridiculous, If I get pneumonia I will make sure my parents sue the Academy,' Alice said.

'You should have put a coat on like the rest of us then,' Stef replied, as she stared at Alice's flimsy tracksuit.

'I'll have you know that this tracksuit is designer and I am not covering it up with a common coat.'

'Well then you can't moan that you're cold.'

Molly and Miss Moffat flew into the arena, Miss Moffat's long black fur coat trailed on the ground as she walked off with Miss Firmfeather.

'Cold enough for you?' Molly grinned, as she jogged on the spot.

'Are we starting soon? I can't feel my toes,' Patricia asked as she shivered.

'Hopefully. And it's a good job that you don't need toes to fly,' she smirked.

Charlotte looked over at Miss Moffat and Miss Firmfeather who were still in deep conversation with each other, before she looked over to the small crowd of students that had gathered to watch. Although there had been a buzz about this competition throughout the Academy, most of the students from the other years were in classes or didn't fancy braving the cold to watch.

Miss Moffat and Miss Firmfeather stopped talking and headed back over to Molly.

'Girls, it is important that you don't let this sudden appearance of cold weather make you lose your focus,' Miss Moffat said.

'Hello girls,' Miss Firmfeather smiled. 'The flying arena has been transformed into a thrilling obstacle course for you all to compete in. I'm sure you're all wondering where the course is, there is an invisibility spell surrounding it that will be lifted once I signal the start of the test. We aim to keep things exciting for you,' she winked.

'I'd advise you to leave your coats here as you will get hot flying around but if you choose to keep them on then that is indeed your choice. Please mount your brooms and you can begin on my whistle.
Remember, you are all aiming to finish in the top five as only these people will receive points for this test.'

'Good luck girls,' she gave them a wide smile, before she placed the whistle that hung around her neck in her mouth.

Charlotte took off her coat and placed it on the ground, she tried to ignore the cold as she got onto her broom and waited for the race to start.

When Miss Firmfeather blew the whistle bright lights whizzed out of it and exploded in the sky in a mass of colors. The whistle continued to echo until of all the girls had cleared the invisible shield, which then vanished so that the spectators could see what was going on.

Hundreds of prickly, tall cacti were zig-zagged in front of them. Margaret was the first to whiz towards them and to begin to weave around the cacti. Alice and Victoria were more hesitant, lingering back on their brooms.

Charlotte exchanged looks with Gerty before they both took off in different directions, swooping their way around them.

Stef had made her way through the zig-zig path quickly and

with ease. She hadn't been prickled once and she wasn't far from the front.

Margaret turned her head and saw how close Stef was behind her. Smirking she flew around the corner and stopped, Stef swooped around the corner just as Margaret swung her broom into the side of her, causing her to tumble backwards into a cactus. Stef screamed out as dozens of prickles embedded themselves into her arm.

'I'll get you for this,' she shouted.

Margaret was quick to fly off and leave Stef there, as she bravely pulled the prickles out of her skin before she got back onto her broom and hurried after Margaret.

As the girls began to clear the cacti, a large, arched, stone bridge came into view. Charlotte wasted no time in zooming towards it, there were several girls in front of her and she knew that she needed to get a move on if she was going to finish in the top five.

There was fencing above the bridge and a black outlined, yellow arrow pointed downwards. Charlotte swooped down and began to fly beneath the bridge, carrying on in a straight line until the signs of daylight in front of her grew clearer.

Suddenly the silhouette of a large moving shape came into view and a troll appeared, growling as it swiped at the girls. Charlotte managed to weave past it and fly out from beneath the bridge. Gerty didn't react quickly enough and the troll grabbed onto her leg and refused to let go. Gerty tried struggling free but the troll was too strong.

'Help,' she shouted but the rest of the girls zoomed past her, none of them stopping to assist her.

'Sorry Gerty,' Patricia said, as she whizzed past her.

Gerty didn't understand why no one had helped her, as she would have stopped and helped them if they'd been in her place. She fought back tears as she again tried to free her leg. The troll continued to growl and wail as time ticked by and Gerty's chances of finishing in the top five grew slimmer.

An idea came into her head and she gripped tightly onto her broom with one hand and with her other hand she went to pull her wand from her pants pocket. Suddenly the troll shook her and she watched in distress as her wand fell through her fingers and clattered onto the ground.

'Please can you let me go, I really don't want to lose this test?' she pleaded with the troll.

The troll looked at her before it stuck its long, white covered tongue out at her and then chortled to itself. Gerty sighed on the knowledge that she wasn't going anywhere soon.

A forest of silky white cobwebs was the next challenge, Alice flew straight into them and squealed as she tried to swipe and shake the cobwebs out of her hair.

'They are only webs Alice, they can't hurt you,' Stef chuckled as she passed her.

Destiny found this challenge easy and had managed to pass Margaret and go into the lead.

'Parvus turbo,' Margaret flicked her wand out at Destiny.

A mini tornado whirled its way around Destiny, causing her

vision to be blurred and causing her to fly straight into a giant golden orb spider's web. The tornado cleared and the spider became visible as it crawled towards Destiny, she let out a loud shriek and struggled to free herself from the web. Margaret smirked as she flew past Destiny, happy that she was now firmly in the lead.

Charlotte and Alice were the next ones to pass Destiny, who was holding her broom out in front of her as a barrier between her and the spider. Eventually the spider scuttled up its web and Destiny hopped back onto her broom and flew off after them.

The cobweb forest ended and the girls found themselves entering a hall of mirrors. Dozens of reflections surrounded them, making them feel giddy. Charlotte had to grip on extra tightly to her broomstick as she began to feel disorientated. She was no longer sure if she was flying upright or upside-down. it was only when her head began to throb that she realized she was upside-down and turned herself around. She rubbed her head as she tried to find her way through the mirror maze.

Demi became so disorientated that she misjudged what was mirror and what wasn't and she flew straight into one of the mirrors and bashed her arm. She groaned under her breath as she rubbed her arm, grateful that she hadn't broken the mirror, as her uncle Syd had done that once and seven-years of bad luck had followed him.

Alice flew past Demi, using her as a guide to dodge the mirrors as she flew around the corner. Demi was quick to fly off after her, although this time she took more care when turning to work out what was mirror and what was space.

Margaret was still in the lead, although Charlotte, Alice and

Demi weren't far behind her. She flew around a corner and saw a huge ornate mirror at the end of the mirrored corridor, the word 'exit' was written above it in bold, flashing letters. She stopped abruptly in front of it and looked around to try and find where the exit was.

Alice and Demi were next to appear and on the mirror with the sign above it they both stopped by Margaret. It was then that Charlotte appeared, she saw Margaret and the others but she also saw the sign, so she took a deep breath before she flew straight at the mirror.

'No, Stop,' Alice shouted.

'Don't do it,' Demi shrieked.

Charlotte ignored them and closed her eyes as she reached the mirror and kept on flying. The glass didn't break, her body didn't bruise, instead she'd flown safely through the mirror and was now in a field full of green-leaved apple trees. It was as warm as a day in late spring and she felt glad that she'd left her coat behind.

The apples were a variety of colors, from dark red to bright orange.

On the ground in front of her were woven baskets and a sign that read: 'To win the test and be the best, pick six apples and in this basket they should rest.'

Quickly she lifted up the basket closely to her and flew off towards the closest tree.

Margaret was furious, she should have known that the mirrored exit was an illusion and not paused in front of it. Now Charlotte was ahead of her and she was stuck with

Alice and Demi. As soon as Charlotte had disappeared through the mirror she had quickly followed her, determined to make sure that she didn't beat her. Margaret was desperate to not only come first in the top five but also to make sure that Charlotte didn't finish in it. This time she wanted Charlie all to herself!

Charlotte had already put her first apple into her basket but as soon as she'd touched the bright green apple the rest of the apples on that tree had vanished. She moved onto the second tree, her sights set on a lilac apple.

Margaret flew after Charlotte, a smirk on her face as she lifted her wand.

'Sempiterno foramen,' she flicked her wand in Charlotte's direction.

Charlotte reached for a second apple and threw it into her basket, she glanced down at it and that's when she double-looked. Her basket was empty and there was a large hole in the bottom of it. She looked over at Margaret who was now on her second apple and knew that she was responsible.

'Reficere,' she pointed her wand at the basket; the hole remained.

'Mutare,' she tried.

The hole remained and worse still, Margaret was now on her fourth apple.

Charlotte bit on the side of her lip as she desperately tried to think up spells that would help her.

'Alice,' she said, as she saw her whiz near her.

Alice was too busy concentrating on collecting apples and she didn't notice Charlotte and flew straight past her.

Charlotte continued to try spells but still the hole remained in her basket. She looked over and saw that Margaret had just flown over the finish line, closely followed by Demi.

One-by-one the rest of the girls crossed the finish line. Charlotte continued to try spells on the basket, even though she knew that she wasn't going to finish in the top five on this test.

'Magicae novis,' she tried.

She looked down to see that the bottom of her woven basket had been restored. Quickly she whizzed from tree to tree, grabbing an array of colorful apples.

After she had crossed the finish line the crowd became visible to her and she could hear the clapping and cheering. She looked at Patricia who was crouched over regaining her breath and then to Alice who was going on and on to Melody about how it was unfair that she hadn't won. Her gaze fell on Margaret, who was looking straight back at her, a devious smirk on her face.

'What happened. You were in the lead then when I crossed the finish line you weren't here?' Stef asked, as she walked over to her.

'A hole mysteriously appeared in my basket,' she sighed.

'No prizes for guessing who was behind that,' Stef looked over at Margaret.

'Where's Gerty?' Charlotte asked.

'Molly had to rescue me from the troll's bridge because you all flew off and left me,' Gerty said, as she walked over to them, with folded arms and dirt smudged cheeks.

'Sorry,' Stef muttered. 'I didn't see that you were in trouble.'

'Patricia did, she flew straight past me.'

'Maybe she didn't realize that you needed help?' Charlotte said.

'Maybe,' Gerty huffed. 'It doesn't matter, I'm sure I'll do better in the next two tests.'

'Of course you will,' Charlotte smiled.

'You both will,' Stef said.

'You didn't finish in the top five?' Gerty gave Charlotte a confused look.

'There was an issue with my basket during the last section of the task.'

'Oh, okay. I'm sure you'll make up for it in the next test, you're a skilled witch.'

'Thanks Gerty, I think that you are a great witch too,' she smiled. 'And you are too Stef.'

'We're all good and we're all going to finish in the top five,' Stef said.

'Course we will,' Gerty smiled.

'I hope so,' Charlotte said under her breath.

'Girls, girls, gather round,' Miss Moffat gestured them forwards. 'A marvellous effort was put in by each and every one of you but as you all know only the first five placed girls will receive points. In fifth place with a score of one point is Destiny.'

Demi cheered and the other girls clapped but Destiny just gave a forced smile. Charlotte took this opportunity to read her mind and found out that Destiny was thinking about how unfair it was that she hadn't come first.

'In fourth place with a score of two points is Stephanie.'

'Well done Stef,' Charlotte patted her on the shoulder.

'Third place with a score of three points is Alice, second place with a score of four points is Demi and taking first place with a score of five points is Margaret. Well done to the top five and for those of you who didn't quite make it, I hope that the remaining tests will show your true potential.'

'Third,' Alice huffed. 'How could I have only come third?'

'Stop moaning, you finished in the top five so I don't know what you have to complain about,' Stef grumbled.

'Third is great Alice and so is fourth,' Gerty smiled at Stef.

Charlotte let out a shiver, as her body suddenly remembered how cold it was out here. She was about to walk off and find her coat when Gerty put an arm around her.

'You'll ace the next test,' she whispered to her.

'Thanks Gerty, so will you.'

Charlotte walked over to her coat that had been placed in a floating pile. She rummaged through the coats and pulled hers free, as she put it on she found herself worrying about the test and how she had managed to mess up the first one. She had been positive around Gerty but she wasn't sure if she believed her own words. She longed to make the top five but she was afraid that she wouldn't and that her chances of seeing Charlie at the competition would completely fade away.

She looked over at Margaret who was standing by herself as she twirled her wand in her hand. Charlotte couldn't resist reading her mind, as she longed to know what she was thinking about.

'It's Thought Thrower time,' she said to herself.

'I'm going to win and I'm going to see Charlie again. He won't be able to resist me and I will claim him as my boyfriend. She doesn't stand a chance,' Margaret thought, as she feigned a smile in Charlotte's direction. 'There's no way that she will make the top five so I won't have to worry about her sticking her nose in.'

'Well done Margaret,' Charlotte forced a smile, as she walked past her.

Charlotte was determined to make the top five and she wasn't going to give up. To stand a chance of making the top five she knew that she had to finish as highly as she could on the next test. She wasn't going to stand by and let Margaret get the better of her and she wasn't going to let her steal Charlie from her.

'Bring on the second test,' she said under her breath.

She walked back over to Stef and Gerty, making sure that she had blocked out all thoughts. She didn't need to read their minds to know that they were her friends and that they would always be there for her. Margaret would always be as smart as she was spiteful, but Charlotte knew that she had something that Margaret would most likely never have. Charlotte had the best friends that she could have asked for and she knew that with them on her side she would be just fine.

***

That afternoon the great hall was set out ready for their second test. Sitting on one side of the long tables were adults that none of the girls had ever seen before.

'As you can see we have some special visitors at the Academy. These are friends of the Academy but they are also normals, they have kindly agreed to take part in this test. You will each go over to a section of one of the tables where a row of three of our guests are sitting and your challenge will be to read their fortunes. Miss Zara is here to explain the rules more clearly,' Miss Moffat said.

'Thank you Miss Moffat,' Miss Zara took a step forward. 'Each of our guests has a crystal ball in front of them. I vant you to look into it and to find out vhat their current job is, vhat their hobby is and vhat they vill be doing in a year's time. Go ahead girls but remember to vait for the signal before you start, as this is a speed race,' she signalled with her hands for them to move.

The girls moved over to the tables and sat behind the first adult in the row of three. Charlotte and Alice both went over to the same long table and sat down next to a different line of normals. Molly was at the head of the table close to Charlotte, her hair braided and fixed into a neat bun.

'Each girl will have someone watching them and you have me,' Molly said to Charlotte, before she waved to Silvia who was stood at the other end of the table near Alice. 'Remember that you need to find out their job, hobby and what they will be doing in a year's time. The aim is to do this accurately and quickly, if you get an answer wrong then you will hear a gong. You can choose to try again or to move onto the next question or person, good luck.'

Charlotte gave her a smile before she looked at the normal woman sitting in front of her. She was about forty, with chin length poker straight hair and she was dressed smartly in a navy suit. Charlotte made sure that she had blocked out all thoughts as she wanted to win this test fairly, also their thoughts would have been an added distraction. She knew that the best way to get the answers she needed was to find them in the crystal ball.

The sound of a squawking bird filled the room and caused dozens of the normals to jump in alarm. Molly gave Charlotte a nod and she quickly placed her hands over the crystal ball and focused on it. An image appeared of the woman, she was stood in front of a classroom with equations written on the blackboard.

'Math teacher,' Charlotte said, smiling when the gong didn't sound.

She looked back into the crystal ball and saw the woman sat in the front row of a theatre.

'Going to the theatre.'

Lastly she saw the woman dressed in leggings and a waterproof jacket, she was carrying a backpack as she walked up a mountain.

'This time next year she will be in Wales, England where she will be visiting family. This day next year she will be climbing Mount Snowdon.'

The normal woman gave Charlotte a smile and she smiled back, before she hopped onto the next seat where a young man was sitting in front of her. She wasted no time in looking into the crystal ball and finding the answers that she needed.

'Chef,' no gong sounded. 'Skiing,' again no gong sounded. 'He will have just bought his first house with his fiancé Christina.'

Charlotte hopped onto the third seat and quickly read the elderly normal gentleman's fortune. Once she had finished Molly made a golden spark shoot out of her wand.

Charlotte looked over at Alice who was reading her second normal's fortune.

Alice said something and the gong sounded, Alice paused briefly before she moved onto the next seat and peered into the crystal ball, desperate to get the answers she needed about the middle-aged woman who sat in front of her.

No one else was even close to finishing and now that Charlotte had finished concentrating on her normals, all she could hear were the other gongs that were sounding off all over the hall.

Gerty was next to finish, she had only made one mistake. She'd seen the man sat on the toilet reading a book and said that his hobby was reading. It turned out that this wasn't really his hobby, he just liked to hide in the bathroom to escape his wife's nagging, his real hobby was taking his grandson to watch their local team play football.

Fortune telling didn't come naturally to Margaret but she'd somehow managed to work out some of the answers from the blurry images she'd conjured up in the crystal ball.

'She's a cleaner,' she said, as she looked up at the smartly dressed woman that was sitting in front of her. The gong sounded and the normal woman gave an insulted look.

'I do apologize,' Miss Moffat said to the woman, after she had rushed over to her. 'Margaret, this is Mrs Davenport, she is head of the normal's university.'

Margaret muttered an apology and blushed before she looked back into the crystal ball.

When the test had finished all the girls gathered in front of Miss Moffat to hear the results.

'Firstly I would like you all to join me in giving a huge thank you to our guests who took time out of their very busy schedules to join us here today,' Miss Moffat flicked her wand and clapping sounds erupted in the hall, which were soon joined by the other girls' claps and cheers. 'Now, for the results. In first place and with one-hundred-percent accuracy,' she arched her eyebrow. 'And who will receive five points is Charlotte.'

The hall erupted in more cheers and Charlotte saw Molly wink at her.

'In second place with ninety-seven percent accuracy and receiving four points is Gertrude. In third place with eighty-percent accuracy and receiving three points is Alice. Fourth place with seventy-three-percent accuracy and receiving two points is Stephanie and finally in fifth place with sixty-five-percent accuracy and receiving one point is Margaret.

Well done to the top five, and to those of you that are disappointed, don't forget that there is still one more test to go. For now, go off and have some free time and may I suggest that you practice your spells. The final test will take place in the yard tomorrow morning straight after breakfast. After this test, our top five will be revealed, which is very exciting. I am eager to observe the final test and to find out which of you girls will be representing the Academy,' she smiled at them before she walked over to the normals and started talking to them.

As the girls followed Molly out of the hall, the sweet smell of hot toffee filled the room. Charlotte glanced back to see that one of the tables was now filled with colorful cakes, snacks and warm drinks for the normals.

'Well done,' Stef said.

'Thanks, you did great too.'

'Third, how could I have come third again?' Alice moaned.

'Third is great Alice, it means that you are in a strong place going into the final test. And you are currently in joint first place with Margaret,' Gerty said.

'I should have come first in both tests,' she muttered, before she walked over to Melody to grumble about her placing to her.

'We are the comeback kids,' Gerty smiled, as she linked arms with Charlotte.

'We sure are.'

Margaret barged past them, an annoyed look on her face.

'Watch it,' Gerty said.

'Whatever,' Margaret snapped.

'I suppose she's just annoyed at her placing,' Gerty shrugged.

'Yeah, probably,' Charlotte replied, unable to hide her smile.

Charlotte and Gerty were currently in fourth and fifth places, they just needed to do well in the spell test and they stood a good chance of making the top five. Charlotte was one step closer to proving that she was an accomplished witch and one step closer to hopefully getting a chance to sort things out with Charlie.

***

It seemed as though the whole school were out in the yard to watch the final test. Lessons had been cancelled for the morning and a floating row of bleachers had been positioned on all sides of the yard.

The first year girls were all lined up on one side of the yard, each of them had a wooden horse in front of them. Across the yard were two large flags with the Academy's crest of two crossing brooms below the letters MMA on them.

'As you can see, you each have a horse in front of you. For your spells test you have to ride your horse over the finish line,' Molly pointed over to the flags. 'To do this you will need to cast a spell on your horse. Begin when you hear the bang of my starter gun, good luck.'

Charlotte and Stef exchanged anxious looks as they waited for the test to begin. Charlotte tried hard to think up a spell to use on her horse but she wasn't sure which one would work best.

BANG, echoed loudly across the arena, followed by

hundreds of bats that flew off across the yard.

'Paulo Equus,' Charlotte aimed her wand at her horse.

A small, greyish-brown animal with a short mane and long ears appeared in front of her.

'Eeaw,' it said, before it nudged its head against her arm and began to chew on her sleeve.

'My sweater's not food,' she shook her head, before she climbed onto the animal.

'Eeaw, eeaw.'
She gently kicked its sides to try and get it to move but it remained where it was.

'Nice donkey,' Margaret snorted over at Charlotte, before she trotted off on a pretty white pony.

Charlotte tried to ignore Margaret and instead patted the donkey.

'Please don't be stubborn, I need to do well in this test.'

'Eeaw,' it said, before it bucked her off.

'What am I going to do with you?' she sighed, as she got back up onto her feet.

The donkey once again moved its head towards her sleeve and as she moved her arm away from it she thought of an idea. She got back onto the donkey and then held out her wand.

'Natantis carota,' she said and a floating carrot appeared in front of the donkey.

The donkey immediately began to move, trying to bite the floating carrot which remained just out of its reach.

At first Demi turned her horse into a rocking horse. She tried to block out the laughter that was coming from the crowd and cast another spell on her horse but this time wheels appeared on her rocking horse. She jumped on it and tried wheeling it forwards, before she cast another spell and this time the wheels spun quickly by themselves, transporting her across the yard.

Alice had turned her horse into a cute Shetland pony but it's little legs were struggling to go very fast.

'Hurry up,' Alice shouted at it.

Destiny had turned her horse into an elegant black stallion and on seeing it the crowd cheered. Once she'd jumped onto it Destiny found that it was far too powerful for her to control and it wandered over to a nearby patch of grass and refused to move from there.

Margaret finished with ease, crossing the line long before anyone else. Next was Alice, who was still shouting at her pony.

Demi whizzed past Stef who was on an angry grey pony, she kicked the pony to get it to move and it flared its nostrils and stopped abruptly, causing her to fall forwards onto its mane. Demi finished in third place and Stef managed to get her pony moving again and finished in fourth.

Charlotte's donkey was still trying to reach the carrot, it was moving forwards but not at a very fast speed. She saw that

Gerty was close by on a Spanish dancing horse, which was trotting her the long way around the arena with its head held high.

'Please, come on,' Charlotte said to the donkey but it carried on forwards at the same pace.

Gerty wasn't far from the finishing line now but her horse had stopped and held its head into the air.

'Please move,' Gerty asked it nicely but it remained still.

Victoria whizzed past Charlotte on a zebra and was just about to cross the finishing line when the zebra got spooked by the cheers and shouts close by. It reared back before it spun around and ran off in the opposite direction, with Victoria clinging onto its mane in fright.

Charlotte passed Gerty just as her horse began to move. She closed her eyes and chewed on the side of her lip as the donkey placed one of its hooves across the finishing line at what appeared to be the same time as Gerty's horse had.

The rest of the girls crossed the finishing line, apart from Destiny who was still trying to move her horse away from the grass. They all gathered around Miss Moffat and excitedly waited for the results.

Charlotte was both excited and nervous. She had the fingers on both of her hands crossed as she eagerly waited for the results. Margaret looked over at her and scowled and Charlotte looked away from her. Still, she could feel Margaret's gaze boring into her.

'I know I'm going to win,' Alice said.

'Get over yourself,' Stef rolled her eyes.

'Congratulations girls, I am most impressed with your progress over the past six months. Today you have demonstrated your abilities and skills and let me tell you that we are impressed...with most of you,' Miss Moffat smiled. 'Remember that only five of you will represent our Academy. And the top five are...in first place is Margaret.'

Margaret squealed in excitement as she jumped on the spot, before she rushed over to Miss Moffat and hugged her. Miss Moffat pulled back and brushed down her coat.

'There's no need for that,' she said and Margaret blushed, before she walked back over to where she'd been standing.

'Second place is Alice.'

'There must be a mistake, surely I came first?' Alice said loudly.

Miss Moffat frowned before she waved her wand at Alice. She carried on trying to talk but no words came out of mouth, so she clasped her hands over her mouth and looked at the ground.

'Third place is Demi, fourth place is Stephanie and lastly in fifth place, with only a fraction of a hoof in it, is...Charlotte. Well done girls, you have shown true promise and skill and I don't doubt that you will do this Academy proud when you compete against the wizard's college.'

Charlotte and Stef hugged each other excitedly but then they looked over at Gerty, who couldn't hide her disappointment.

'I'm sorry Gerty, it was so close,' Charlotte said.

'You still did well, your horse was really good,' Stef said.

'Thanks guys,' Gerty forced a smile. 'But it's okay, you both did great and deserve to be in the top five,' she hugged them both.

They pulled apart and stood in silence for a few moments.

'Hopefully Charlie will make the wizard's team too,' Gerty winked at Charlotte.

'Hopefully,' she smiled.

'I'm positive he will, although you can't go all gooey-eyed as there's a trophy to be won,' she grinned.

***

The day of the competition arrived and the five girls to make the team flew with Molly over to Alexander's College.

Dale was there to greet them and he led them through the hallways of the castle and into the empty hall. There were seats set out on each side of the stage and Dale gestured for them to sit there.

'It's very quiet, when do you think the boy's will arrive?' Stef whispered to Charlotte.

'Why am I sitting on this end?' Alice huffed. 'They will think that I came last.'

'Who cares,' Stef replied, rolling her eyes.

Alexander appeared on the stage in a royal blue suit.

'Molly, always a pleasure,' he leaned over so that he could kiss her hand.

'Alexander, Miss Moffat sends her regards and hopes that you won't miss the trophy too much,' Molly grinned.

'Well, we shall see about that.'

'Girls, no doubt you are wondering who you will be competing against? Well wonder no more,' he whistled and five boys wearing long black capes and floppy wizard hats appeared on the stage.

Charlotte looked eagerly at the boys but she couldn't tell if one of them was Charlie.

'The first member of our team,' Alexander gestured to the boy on the end of the row...'

Charlotte held her breath as she watched the boy take off his hat.

'Is William.' Polite applause greeted this decision.

'In second place...is Patrick. ' Once again, people clapped their hands.

'Third was John.'

'Fourth place goes to Michael.'

Both Charlotte and Margaret were shocked, their chins dropped at the thought of missing out on seeing Charlie.

'And the final competitor to face the girls is'...he seemed to take an eternity to say the last name... 'Charlie.'

On seeing his brown hair and sparkling eyes both Charlotte and Margaret jumped out of their seats and cheered loudly. All eyes in the room turned to the two girls.

Charlie looked over at Charlotte and smiled, then he winked at Margaret.

'Well, this is going to be interesting,' Stef whispered to Alice.

Who will win the battle to claim Charlie's heart?

Find out in Witch School Book 4
Out NOW!

Thank you so much for reading Witch School 3.
If you could leave a review, that would greatly help me to
continue to write more books.
Thank you!!!!!
Katrina xx

More great books for you...

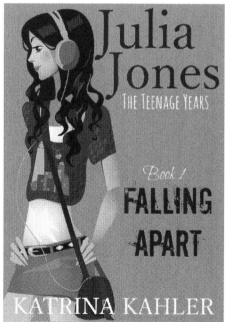

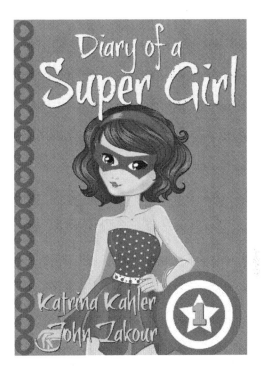

Diary of a
Super Girl

Katrina Kahler
John Zakour

Diary of an
ALMOST COOL WITCH

Book 1

Bill & Kaz Campbell

24330902R00071

Printed in Great Britain
by Amazon